P9-AQS-639

THE CAT WHO WENT UP THE CREEK

Also by Lilian Jackson Braun

THE CAT WHO COULD READ BACKWARDS
THE CAT WHO ATE DANISH MODERN
THE CAT WHO TURNED ON AND OFF
THE CAT WHO SAW RED
THE CAT WHO PLAYED BRAHMS
THE CAT WHO PLAYED POST OFFICE
THE CAT WHO KNEW SHAKESPEARE
THE CAT WHO SNIFFED GLUE
THE CAT WHO WENT UNDERGROUND
THE CAT WHO TALKED TO GHOSTS
THE CAT WHO LIVED HIGH
THE CAT WHO KNEW A CARDINAL
THE CAT WHO MOVED A MOUNTAIN
THE CAT WHO WASN'T THERE
THE CAT WHO WENT INTO THE CLOSET
THE CAT WHO CAME TO BREAKFAST
THE CAT WHO BLEW THE WHISTLE
THE CAT WHO SAID CHEESE
THE CAT WHO TAILED A THIEF
THE CAT WHO SANG FOR THE BIRDS
THE CAT WHO SAW STARS
THE CAT WHO ROBBED A BANK
THE CAT WHO SMELLED A RAT

THE CAT WHO HAD 14 TALES
(SHORT STORY COLLECTION)

LILIAN JACKSON BRAUN

THE
CAT WHO
WENT UP
THE CREEK

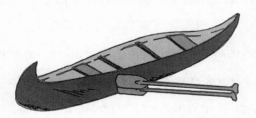

BOOKSPAN LARGE PRINT EDITION

G.P. PUTNAM'S SONS
NEW YORK

This Large Print Edition, prepared especially for Bookspan, contains the complete, unabridged text of the original Publisher's Edition.

G. P. Putnam's Sons
Publishers Since 1838
a member of
Penguin Putnam Inc.
375 Hudson Street
New York, NY 10014

ISBN 0-7394-2329-0

Printed in the United States of America

Book design by Patrice Sheridan

Front jacket images of squirrels and gold nuggets
© Index Stock Imagery

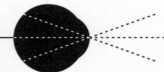

This Large Print Book carries the Seal of Approval of N.A.V.H.

Dedicated to Earl Bettinger,
The Husband Who . . .

THE CAT WHO WENT UP THE CREEK

chapter one

It was Skeeter Week in Moose County, 400 miles north of everywhere. Armies of young enthusiastic mosquitoes rose from woodland bogs and deployed about the county, harassing tourists. Permanent residents were never bothered. And, after a while, even newcomers developed an immunity, attributed to minerals in the drinking water and in the soil that grew such flavorful potatoes. As for the summer people, they bought quantities of insect repellent and went on praising the perfect weather, the wonderful fishing, and the ravishing natural beauty of Moose County.

One morning in mid-June a columnist for the *Moose County Something* was working against deadline, writing his annual thousand-word salute to Skeeter Week.

With tongue in cheek he reported readers' exaggerated claims: A farmer in Wildcat had trained a corps of skeeters to buzz him awake every morning in time for milking. A music teacher in Pickax City had a pet skeeter that buzzed Mendelssohn's "Spinning Song."

He was no backwoods journalist. He was James Mackintosh Qwilleran, former crime writer for major newspapers Down Below, as the locals called all states except Alaska. A freak inheritance had brought him north to Pickax, the county seat (population 3,000). It also made him the richest man in the northeast central United States. (It was a long story.)

He cut a striking figure as he went about, interviewing and making friends for the paper. He was fiftyish, tall, well built, with an enviable head of graying hair and a pepper-and-salt moustache of magnificent proportions. But there was more to the man than an instantly recognizable moustache; he had brooding eyes and a sympathetic mien and a willingness to listen that encouraged confidences. Yet, his friends, readers, and fellow citizens had come to realize that the sober aspect masked a genial personality and sense of humor. And everyone knew that he lived alone in a converted apple barn, with two Siamese cats.

Qwilleran wrote his column, "Straight from the Qwill Pen," on an old electric typewriter at the barn, closely supervised by his male cat. As he ripped the last page out of the machine, Kao K'o Kung, with an internal growl, let him know the phone was going to ring.

It rang, and a familiar woman's voice said anxiously, "Sorry to bother you, Qwill."

"No bother. I've just finished—"

"I need to talk to you privately," she interrupted, "while my husband is out of town."

Qwilleran had a healthy curiosity and a journalist's taste for intrigue. "Where's he gone?"

"To Bixby, for plumbing fixtures. It may be foolish of me, but—"

"Don't worry. I'll be there in a half hour."

"Come to the cottage in the rear."

Lori and Nick Bamba were the young couple who had come to his rescue when he was a greenhorn from Down Below getting bitten by mosquitoes. She was a small-town postmaster then; he was chief engineer at the state prison. They had two ambitions: to raise a family and to be innkeepers.

When Qwilleran had an opportunity to recommend them for the new Nutcracker Inn located in Black Creek, he was happy to do so. In a way, he felt like the godfather of the Nutcracker. If he had not been the sole heir of Aunt Fanny Klingenschoen (who was not even related to him) . . . And if he had not been totally overwhelmed by the size of the bequest (billions) and the responsibility it entailed . . . And if he had not established the Klingenschoen Foundation to use the money for the good of the community . . . And if the K Fund had not purchased the old Limburger mansion to refurbish as a country inn . . .

Such were his ruminations as he drove the miles to Black Creek, a virtual ghost town until the Nutcracker Inn brought it back to life. The renovation had won national publicity; some well-known names had appeared on the guest register; new shops were opening in the quaint little downtown.

Qwilleran had seen the Victorian house when the last eccentric Limburger was alive. A section of the ornamental iron fence had been sold to a passing stranger; a broken window was a Halloween trick when the old man refused to treat; bricks from the crumbling steps were used to throw at stray dogs. In Qwilleran's opinion, the only upbeat feature was a cuckoo clock in the front hall, its crazy bird popping out and announcing the time with monotonous cheer.

Now, approaching Black Creek, he planned his strategy. In Moose County, where everyone knew the make and model of everyone's vehicle, his own five-year-old brown van was especially conspicuous. It would hardly do to be seen calling on the innkeeper's wife while the innkeeper was in Bixby buying plumbing supplies. So the brown van was parked in the main lot of the inn with the luncheon guests, after which the driver ambled about the grounds feeding the squirrels. Not having any peanuts, he had brought cocktail nuts, and the squirrels showed no objection to pecans and cashews, slightly salted.

The Lori Bamba who admitted him to the cottage was not the sunny personality he had known. The golden braids coiled around her head seemed drab, and her eyes were not as blue. She offered him coffee and a black walnut cookie, and he accepted.

"How are the Bambas' brilliant brats?" he asked to add a light touch.

"The boys are in summer camp, and Lovey is with her grandma in Mooseville. We get together Sundays."

"That's good. So what is the serious matter on your mind?"

"Well . . . I always thought innkeeping would be my kind of work: meeting people, making them happy, providing a holiday atmosphere. Instead I feel gloomy."

"Is your health okay?"

"At my last physical my doctor said I'd live to be a hundred and ten." She said it without a smile. "The funny thing is—when I go to Mooseville on Sundays or into Pickax on errands, I feel normal. I think there's something depressing about the building itself! I've always been sensitive to my environment, and I believe the theory that old houses absorb the personality of those who've lived there."

He nodded. "I've heard that!" He avoided saying whether he believed it.

"Nick says I'm being silly. He says it's all in my head. It's a grand old building, and the redecorating is fabulous, but I feel a dark cloud hanging over the premises."

What could he say? He thought of the Dunfield house at the beach, where a man had been murdered. Realty agents could neither rent nor sell it, although its unsavory past had been suppressed. He said, "I wish there were something I could do. I'd be willing to spend a few days here— to see if I pick up any adverse vibrations."

"Would you, Qwill?" she cried. "You could have a suite on the top floor and bring the cats. You'd be our guest!"

"No, no! The story would be that I'm researching material for my column. All charges would go on my expense account. What meals are available?"

"Breakfast and dinner. We have an excellent chef—from Palm Springs. Also, the suites have a small refrigerator and a coffee maker. Would you like to see one of them?"

"Won't be necessary. I had the grand tour when the inn opened last fall. Is the black cat still here?"

"Nicodemus? Oh, yes! The guests love him; he's so sweet in spite of his wicked eyes!" He was sleek and black with the most unusual eyes; they were triangular and had a stare like a laser beam. "He's our rodent control officer," Lori said with some of her old enthusiasm. "He doesn't catch mice; he just terrifies them. Do you like canoeing, Qwill? We have a few canoes available down at the creek."

In his younger days Qwilleran had often thought, If I can't play second base for the Chicago Cubs, or write for *The New York Times,* or act on the Broadway stage . . . I'd like to be an investigator. And now even so nebulous a mystery as Lori's "dark cloud" piqued his curiosity. Furthermore . . .

Qwilleran relished a frequent change of address. His early experience as a globe-trotting correspondent had given him a chronic case of wanderlust. The Black Creek venture would be timely; the chief woman in his life was leaving on vacation. Polly Duncan, director of the Pickax public library, planned to tour museum villages on the East Coast in the company of her sister, who lived in Cincinnati. Qwilleran wondered about these sisterly flings. In Canada the previous year they had met a highly personable Quebec professor, and he had been corresponding with Polly ever since . . . in French! She said it helped her brush up on her idioms.

Qwilleran would drive her to the airport in the morning, but tonight there would be a farewell dinner in the Mackintosh Room at the hotel.

As soon as they were seated, he asked

the usual fatuous questions. "Are you all packed? Are you excited?"

"I hate to leave Brutus and Catta, but there's a cat-sitter in the neighborhood who'll come in twice a day to give them food and attention. This morning I wrote a limerick about Catta while I was shower-ing: A female feline named Catta / is get-ting fatta and fatta / but she's pretty and purry / and funny and furry / so what does an ounce or two matta?"

"I couldn't have done 'betta' myself," he said, with apologies. "If we announce an-other limerick contest this summer, will you be one of the judges?"

"I'd love to! Meanwhile, what are you go-ing to do while I'm away?"

"Read trashy novels and give wild par-ties, if I can find anyone who likes wild par-ties. . . . But seriously, I plan to spend a couple of weeks at the Nutcracker Inn in search of new material for my column."

"I wish you were coming with me, Qwill."

"Maybe next year, but *no museums*! I get all the education I want on the 'Qwill Pen' beat."

"We could go to the Italian hill country

and read poetry, far from the madding crowd."

"The madding crowd is everywhere these days, Polly—taking snapshots and buying postcards. And by the way, when you send me postcards, bear in mind that the picture on the front is less important than the message on the back! More news! More news!"

His own words would ring in his ears for the next two weeks; Polly always cooperated with zeal.

But first Qwilleran had to get her to the airport for the 8:00 A.M. shuttle flight to Minneapolis. After tearful goodbyes to Brutus and Catta and a race to the airport, the flight was delayed because the pilot of the shuttle had not arrived. According to the airport manager, the pilot's baby-sitter was ill, and she was having difficulty finding a substitute. Eventually she arrived and passengers were reassured that they would make their connections.

When the plane finally taxied to the runway, lifted off and disappeared into the sky, the groundlings watched it go, as if witnesses to a miracle.

On the way home Qwilleran pulled off the highway to make some phone calls. Moose County was the first in the state to prohibit use of a cell phone while operating a vehicle. The county commissioners expected enough revenue from traffic tickets to build a soccer stadium.

First he called Andrew Brodie, the Pickax chief of police. "Andy, I'll be out of town for a few weeks, and I have a bottle of twelve-year-old single-malt Scotch that's too good to leave around for burglars. How about coming over for a nightcap?"

The chief, always interested in crime prevention, said he would be there at 10:00 P.M.

Next Qwilleran phoned Junior Goodwinter, the young managing editor of the *Moose County Something.* "Junior, I'll be faxing the copy for my next few columns. I'll be crossing the Egyptian desert by dromedary."

"So soon? You just got back from doing Paris by skateboard!"

"I have to keep my column fresh, you know."

"Don't let it get too fresh," Junior warned. "We have a conservative reader-ship."

On the way home, Qwilleran made a mental list of things to do and items to pack for the trek to Black Creek, half an hour from home:

Notify post office.
Notify attorney.
Notify janitorial service.
Empty refrigerator.
Pack clothes, writing materials, books, magazines.
Pack cats' commode and two large bags of cat litter, two plates and two water bowls, vitamin drops, grooming essentials, Koko's harness and leash, old paisley necktie.
Take trail bike and Silverlight.

The Siamese were waiting for him apprehensively; they knew! They sensed a change in their comfortable lives.

"You're going on vacation!" Qwilleran assured them. "You're to be guests at a glamorous inn that has room service and a chef from Palm Springs—or Palm Beach. There's a resident cat named Nicodemus who's very friendly. And you can even go up the creek in a canoe."

The Siamese, who subscribed to the home-sweet-home ethic, were always vastly inconvenienced by his restlessness, however. Silent and motionless and disapproving, they sat in a shaft of sunlight slanting through a high barn window. It made the pale fur bodies glisten, and their dark brown masks and ears stand out in sharp and defiant contrast. (Brown legs and tails were tucked out of sight.)

"Well, for your information, you're going anyway," Qwilleran told them.

Yum Yum, the gentle little female, squeezed her eyes noncommittally. Koko, the lordly male, who knew his name was really Kao K'o Kung, slapped the floor with his tail. When their midday snack was placed in the feeding station, they ignored it until Qwilleran was out of the room.

    In the afternoon he reported to the art center, where he was to help judge best of show in a new exhibit opening Sunday. They would be self-portraits by local artists. He would be first to admit he knew nothing about art, but he knew it was his name they wanted on the judges' panel—not his expertise. The manager of the art center had swiveled her eyes at him; Barb Ogilvie had a talent for using her eyeballs to get what she wanted. She had neglected to tell him that the portraitists were all third-graders.

"The purpose of this event," she explained to the assembled judges, "is to introduce the art center to families who might not otherwise come here. They will be voting for their favorite and having punch and cookies. We hope to make friends."

The judges' choice as best-of-show was a portrait of a blond girl in a pink dress, done in pastels.

Barb said to Qwilleran, "Will you attend the opening?"

"Sorry. I'll be in Black Creek on assignment, but I think it would be nice if you'd have dinner with me sometime afterward—at the Nutcracker Inn." One of his chief pleasures was taking someone—anyone—to dinner at a good restaurant.

"I'd love it!" she cried, swiveling her eyes. No one ever said no to Qwilleran's dinner invitations.

So far, so good, Qwilleran thought. Now came the hard part: relocating two opinionated cats who disliked a change of address. His strategy would be one of stealth, carried out in three separate operations.

First, while waiting for Andy, he took the Siamese to the screened gazebo overlooking the garden. Nature's night noises would steal their attention from activity in the barnyard, where two bikes were being lashed to the interior of a van.

At 10:00 P.M. Andrew Brodie arrived at the barn—a big burly Scot with the authority of a police chief and the swagger of a bagpiper. He was both. "So where you goin' this time?" he demanded.

"Black Creek—staying at the Nutcracker Inn, scrounging material for the column."

"What'll you do with the cats?"

"Take them along." Qwilleran was setting out a cheese board with Cheddar, smoked Gouda and Stilton. Andy liked to sit at the snack bar and cut chunks and slices for himself. "Your daughter did a great job of refurbishing that old building, Andy."

"Yep, it was pretty much of a dump."

"It'll be in a national magazine next month, and I hear Fran is getting offers from Chicago and elsewhere."

"Yep, she's doin' all right." Brodie said it ruefully, and Qwilleran recalled that he was talking to a typical old north-country father who considered a career less desirable than family life. He changed the subject. "Andy, did you know old Gus Limburger?"

"Sure did! He was a crazy old codger. He went around asking women to marry him and run his mansion like a boarding house. He asked young and old, ugly and pretty, married and single. We had so many complaints, we threatened to charge him with disturbing the peace." Andy slapped his thigh and hooted. "Lois Inchpot chased him out of her restaurant with a rolling pin! That was after he came back from living in Germany for a while. I was working for the sheriff then, and the Limburger mansion was one of our regular stops on patrol. A real estate office paid the taxes and kept the grass cut, and we reported vandalism to them. People called it a haunted house. That was twenty-thirty years ago. . . . Ever meet old Gus?"

"I tried to interview him but he was too eccentric. He sat on the porch, throwing stones at stray dogs, and he was chasing a dog when he tripped over a loose brick in the front steps. The fall killed him."

"Everybody was surprised to learn he had a daughter in Germany. I bet she was only too glad to sell everything to the K Fund."

"Freshen your drink, Andy?" Qwilleran asked.

"A wee dram. . . . Say, d'you know Doc Abernethy? Lives in Black Creek. Pediatrician. Takes care of my grandkids."

Soberly Qwilleran said, "No, I don't know him. I take my family to the vet."

His guest dismissed that remark with a grunt. "Doc has a story to tell that changed his life."

"From what to what?"

"You look him up and ask him. He tells a good story—and all true, he swears."

"He writes a good letter to the editor," Qwilleran admitted.

"Good citizen. Gets involved." The chief looked at his watch, and drained his glass. "Gotta pick m'wife up at the church."

His departure ushered in the second stage of Qwilleran's strategy. He brought the cats in from the gazebo, half-drugged with nocturnal lights, and then he gave them a larger-than-usual bedtime snack. They staggered up the ramp to the third balcony, and Qwilleran put a wildlife video (without the sound) on their VCR. Yum Yum was asleep before he closed the door, and Koko was swaying noticeably in front of the screen.

Congratulating himself, Qwilleran spent the next hour in feverish but silent activity—padding around in house slippers,

packing luggage and boxes, quietly opening and closing doors and drawers, being
careful not to drop anything.

Everything was going as planned. The
chief had promised to keep an eye on the
barn in his absence. Three weeks' needs for
man and cats were successfully stacked inside the kitchen door, ready for a pre-break-
fast getaway, when Qwilleran turned off the
lights and went to his suite on the first balcony. Before he could open the door, his
ears were assaulted by a prolonged, high-
decibel howl in two-part harmony from the
upper precincts. He cringed. It seemed to
say, You can't fool us, you chump!

There was nothing more he could do or
say; they would have to howl until their
batteries ran down. Then it occurred to
him to reread a chapter in a book he was
writing. A collection of Moose County leg-
ends, it was to be titled *Short & Tall Tales.*

THE LEGEND OF THE RUBBISH HEAP

In the mid-nineteenth century, when
Moose County was beginning to boom, it

was a Gold Rush without the gold. There were veins of coal to be mined, forests to be lumbered, granite to be quarried, land to be developed, fortunes to be made. It would become the richest county in the state.

In 1859 two penniless youths from Germany arrived by schooner, by way of Canada. On setting foot on the foreign soil, they looked this way and that to get their bearings, and both saw it at the same time! A piece of paper money in a rubbish heap! Without stopping to inquire its value, they tore it in half to signify their partnership. It would be share and share alike from then on.

Their names were Otto Wilhelm Limburger and Karl Gustav Klingenschoen. They were fifteen years old.

Labor was needed. They hired on as carpenters, worked long hours, obeyed orders, learned everything they could, used their wits, watched for opportunities, took chances, borrowed wisely, cheated a little, and finally launched a venture of their own.

By the time they were in their thirties, Otto and Karl dominated the food-and-shelter industry. They owned all the rooming houses, eating places and travelers' inns along the shoreline. Only then did they marry: Otto, a God-fearing woman named Gretchen; Karl, a fun-loving woman nicknamed Minnie. At the double wedding the friends pledged to name their children after each other. They hoped for boys, but girls could be named Karla and Wilhelmina. Thus the two families became even more entwined . . . until rumors about Karl's wife started drifting back from the waterfront. When Karl denied the slander, Otto trusted him.

But there was more! One day Karl approached his partner with an idea for expanding their empire. They would add saloons, dance halls, and female entertainment of various kinds. . . . Otto was outraged! The two men argued. They traded insults. They even traded a few blows and, with noses bleeding, tore up the fragments of currency that had been in their pockets since the miracle of the rubbish heap.

Karl proceeded on his own and did extremely well, financially. To prove it, he built a fine fieldstone mansion in Pickax City, across from the courthouse. In retaliation Otto imported masons and woodworkers from Europe to build a brick palace in the town of Black Creek. How the community reacted to the two architectural wonders should be mentioned. The elite of the county vied for invitations to sip tea and view Otto's black walnut woodwork; Karl and Minnie sent out invitations to a party and no one came.

When it was known that the brick mansion would be the scene of a wedding, the best families could talk of nothing else. The bride was Otto's only daughter. He had arranged for her to marry a suitable young man from the Goodwinter family; the date was set. Who would be invited? Was it true that Otto had taken his daughter before a magistrate and legally changed her name from Karla to Elsa? It was true. Elsa's dower chest was filled with fine household linens and intimate wedding finery. Gifts were being delivered in the best carriages in town. Seamstresses were working overtime on costumes for the wedding guests. Gowns for the bridal party were being shipped from Germany. Suppose there were a storm at sea! Suppose they did not arrive in time!

Then, on the very eve of the nuptials, Otto's daughter eloped with the youngest son of Karl Klingenschoen!

Shock, embarrassment, sheer horror and the maddening suspicion that Karl and Minnie had promoted the defection— all these emotions combined to affect Otto's mind.

As for the young couple, there were rumors that they had gone to San Francisco. When the news came, a few years later, that the young couple had lost their lives in the earthquake, Elsa's father had no idea who they were.

Karl and Minnie lived out their lives in the most splendid house in Pickax, ignored by everyone of social standing. Karl never knew that his immense fortune was wiped out, following the financial crash of 1929.

Toward the end of the century, Otto's sole descendent was an eccentric who sat on the porch of the brick palace and threw stones at dogs.

Karl's sole descendant was Fanny

Klingenschoen, who recovered her grand-father's wealth ten times over.

Eventually the saga of the two families took a curious twist. The Klingenschoen Foundation has purchased two properties from the Limburger estate: the mansion in Black Creek and the hotel in Pickax. The former has become the Nutcracker Inn; the latter is now the Mackintosh Inn. The "legend of the rubbish heap" has come full circle.

When Qwilleran finished reading, he thought, That old building has earned a dark cloud. . . . We shall see!

chapter two

Qwilleran's strategy for the morning departure was to take his traveling companions by surprise: Up early—no breakfast—bundle them into the carrier before their eyes are open—talk fast— take off! He talked about everything to his silent passengers—sullen or stunned, it was not clear.

"This is no worse than going to the vet for your annual physical. And the good news is, you don't get the needle or ther- mometer. You'll be pampered guests, liv- ing on the third floor in a room with a view. There are plenty of crows and squirrels for entertainment. And there's a resident cat with an interesting personality. You won't meet socially, but you can sniff each other through the door. And Koko can go for walks down to the creek to watch the trout jumping out of the water."

The male cat was always ready to buckle up and go for a ride on Qwilleran's shoulder. The female missed the point entirely; when buckled up she flopped down on her side and expected to be dragged like a toy wagon.

Qwilleran assumed the role of tour director, telling them more than they wanted to know, but it was the timbre and resonance of his voice that pacified them. Still he told them how Black Creek had gone from a thriving pioneer town to a bed of ashes in the Great Fire of 1869 and how it was restored to even greater importance, with an opera house and the Limburger mansion. Then the mines closed and the forests were lumbered out, and Black Creek became a ghost town.

When Qwilleran stopped for breath, a well-timed "Yow!" indicated that Koko was listening. Yum Yum had been lulled to sleep.

The van arrived at the side door of the inn, and a young man rushed out, saying, "Welcome to Nutcracker Inn! You must be

Mr. Qwilleran. I'm Trent. I'll take you up to the third floor front, our best suite!"

He was one of the Moose County Community College students enrolled in the school's restaurant and hotel management program. They worked part time as porters, servers, dishwashers and house-keepers—happy to get experience in their chosen fields and brimming with energy and enthusiasm.

Trent loaded everything into the new elevator. As it rose slowly and smoothly, he said, "You got kitties?"

"Yow!" came a howl so loud and piercing that the elevator jolted.

"Yikes! What kind of animal is that?"

"A male Siamese," Qwilleran said. "It offends him to be called a kitty. He's a cat."

"Sorry, cat! . . . Does he bite?"

"Only MCCC students. Watch your vocabulary!"

"What's his name?"

"Kao K'o Kung . . . Koko to you."

 As soon as they had moved in, Qwilleran opened the door of the carrier, and two cautious cats emerged shoulder to shoulder, looking left and right.

He said, "Welcome to the Nutcracker Suite!"

Yum Yum sniffed the foreign carpet thoroughly, as usual. Koko walked directly to a closed door in the front corner of the sitting room. Did he know it led to the turret? He liked being high up, looking down. Obligingly Qwilleran turned the old cast-brass doorknob. It was locked. "Treat!" he announced and served two plates of food before phoning the office about the locked door.

"Nick Bamba speaking," said a cheery voice.

"Nick, this is Qwill. We've just arrived and—"

"Welcome to Nutcracker Inn! Glad to have you here! By the way—" He lowered his voice. "Lori told me she spoke to you about the 'dark cloud.' I don't go for that psychic stuff myself. How about you, Qwill?"

"I try to keep an open mind."

"Just the same, I wish you'd talk to her and straighten her out. She'll listen to you. . . . How do you like your suite? Everything okay?"

"Except for a door that's locked. It seems to lead to the turret."

"Oh, yeah . . . that one. I've searched all over for a key. No luck."

"Why don't you pick the lock? You know how. Koko wants to go up there for a bird's-eye view."

"Good idea, Qwill. I'll go right up," Nick said.

"I'm going down—for breakfast. The cats will be shut up in the bedroom."

Qwilleran walked slowly downstairs, admiring the carved staircase of traditional black walnut—deep chocolate brown with purplish veining. In the lobby he was greeted by an effervescent young woman. "Welcome to Nutcracker Inn! You must be Mr. Qwilleran. I'm Cathy, assistant manager on weekends. We're all glad to have you here. We love the 'Qwill Pen' column and wish you wrote it every day. My aunt was a winner in your haiku contest. Are you having breakfast with us? Sit anywhere."

"Thank you, and I'd like to reserve a

table for three for dinner this evening. Six-thirty."

It had been the drawing room of the mansion, and there was more of the lavishly carved woodwork—in the mantle and around doors and windows. Wall spaces that had once been covered with Victorian wallpaper were now painted pale coral; at the dinner hour there would be tablecloths to match. It was a friendly room, and a friendly server took his order: a ramekin of corned beef hash with poached egg, served with black walnut muffins.

"My name is Bella. May I serve you coffee? I've just brewed a fresh pot."

He had brought Friday's paper to read, and every time he read a sentence and took a sip of coffee, Bella added another splash to his cup. "You're going to adore this ramekin," she gushed when she served it. "I had one just before I came on duty." Then she hovered about, in case he should want another muffin or more coffee.

Suddenly Nick Bamba appeared at his table. "Good news! We got the turret door open!"

"Sit down," Qwilleran invited. "Have a cup of coffee. They have an oversupply in the kitchen."

"Guess what we found! A circular staircase carved out of a single black walnut log!"

"How would it photograph?"

"Great! There's some old furniture crowded in there, but it could be moved. And the room needs cleaning badly."

"Then, full speed ahead, Nick. The publisher of the paper is my dinner guest tonight. I want to show it to him."

Nick jumped to his feet. "Consider it done!" And rushed out of the room. He was famous for doing everything *right now*!

Qwilleran finished the ramekin and then read his newspaper with yet another cup of coffee. On the editorial page there was a letter to the editor from Black Creek, written by Brodie's friend, Doc Abernethy. He wrote a good letter.

To the Editor—By what logic does the U.S. Postal Service treat remote rural communities like the suburbs of large cities? In a high-handed move that can be considered only as unthinking, the post offices of small towns and villages are being closed and new ones are being built in the cornfields and sheep pastures.

By tradition, and for reasons of common sense, the village post office is more than a place to buy stamps and mail packages. It is the hub of the community. Clustered around it are the grocery, drugstore, hardware, bank, coffeehouse and barbershop—depending upon and supporting each other. In the post office you bump into your neighbor and compare notes on the weather, crops, flocks, family well-being, and problems of all kinds.

What is happening now? The post offices of Little Hope and Campbelltown were the first to go. A single facility was built in a virtual wasteland in between. Soon the Little Hope Bank and the Campbelltown grocery moved out there. Gradually other businesses were forced to follow suit. Result? The downtown of each village is a ghost town. And where two grocers and barbers were earning a living, there is only one of each.

Meanwhile the price of postage goes up. Families drive farther for everyday goods and services. And what we have is a strip mall in the wilderness. Plans are under way to destroy Fishport and Black Creek. Chipmunk and Squunk Corners will be next. Who is making a profit from this maneuver? I smell a rat!

The letter was signed by Bruce Abernethy, M.D., the friend of Andrew Brodie. The chief was nobody's fool! If he said the doctor had once had a close encounter with a wood spirit, Qwilleran was ready to believe it—or, at least, investigate it.

After breakfast, Qwilleran went for a walk about the grounds wearing shorts and sandals and a baseball cap. His moustache was recognized everywhere, of course. As goodwill ambassador for the *Moose County Something,* he responded to women's admiring looks with a courteous nod and to men's greetings with a salute. He knew he looked good in a baseball cap.

And yet, as a newcomer to the north country, he had wondered about the great number of visored caps on males in all walks of life. Then an agricultural agent told him, "Things fall off trees and out of the sky (don't ask what), and a wise head keeps covered." So he began his collection of baseball caps: hunter orange, red, black, yellow, and a new pale coral with an *N* logo.

So, matching the walls and tablecloths of the inn, Qwilleran set out to explore the grounds. The renovated mansion stood three stories high, with the third floor behind a mansard roof, and the turret rose from the southwest corner, adding a fourth-floor vantage point. Bricks were laid horizontally, vertically, diagonally and in herringbone borders—some protruding slightly to add texture to the façade. This feature was not lost on the squirrel population; with their bold claws they could run up the side of the mansion as easily as they ran up a tree. The management discouraged this activity, although guests found it endearing and reached for their cameras. Windows were tall and narrow, with inserts of stained glass. There was also a brick rampart across the front of the building—the launching pad from which Gustav Limburger had fired missiles at stray dogs. Guests preferred to sit on a paved patio at the rear and feed the squirrels. There were no expanses of neatly clipped lawn. This was a country inn, and the K Fund had specified natural landscaping: ground cover, shrubs, hedges, mammoth boulders, specimen trees, wildflowers, and herbs.

The land sloped gently down to the creek, meandering through wild gardens and the black walnut grove that had given the inn its name. Squirrels performed their acrobatics, and guests sat on park benches and fed them peanuts.

Upstream the creek cut through a dense forest that had been placed in legal conservancy by the Klingenschoen Foundation, forever to remain a wilderness performing natural services for the environment.

Downstream were five rustic cabins facing the water, which the inn offered for rent by the week, month or season. They were widely spaced and each had a screened porch overlooking the creek.

Qwilleran stood on the bank and marveled at the serenity of this waterway that had been a raging torrent in lumbering days, when logs were floated downstream during the spring thaw. Now it was about fifty feet wide—and placid as a pond. If Polly were there, he reflected, she would recite Wordsworth: *The river glideth at his own sweet will,* but she would change the gender of the pronoun to *her.*

As he watched, the only ripples were in concentric circles when another trout leaped to catch another skeeter . . . and a V-shaped wake as a duck moved effortlessly through the water, followed by half a dozen ducklings leaving their own little wakes.

The five rustic cabins on the bank of the creek were about a hundred feet apart, each with a screened porch overlooking the water, each with parking space at the rear. Walking along the footpath at water's edge, Qwilleran checked them out in the systematic way he had.

Cabin One—Small white car with Florida

plates. Cabin windows open. Woman singing a number from a Gilbert & Sullivan opera—live, not a recording.

Cabin Two—No vehicle. TV going full blast. In the front yard, young boy throwing rocks at ducks. Qwilleran chided him, and he ran indoors, where a shrill voice scolded him for talking to strangers. Qwilleran thought, City types!

Cabin Three—New SUV in parking lot. Stereo playing Schubert's "Trout" Quintet. Did he also compose a "Duck" Sonata, "Squirrel" Concerto and "Skeeter" Rhapsody?

Cabin Four—No car. Large woman sitting on porch. He said, "Beautiful day!" She only glared at him. He decided she was deaf.

Cabin Five—No sign of life.

Farther downstream was a boat shed offering canoes and outboards for hire . . . and, in the distance, the picturesque Old Stone Bridge now used only by fishermen.

Back at the inn he found extension ladders leaning against the turret and window-washers hard at work.

In the lobby Nick signaled him. "The turret room in your suite is spic and span, but your cats are raising the roof. They don't like being shut up in the bedroom."

Koko's declamatory yowl and Yum Yum's shriek could be heard in the lobby. Qwilleran ran upstairs and released them from their prison. "Please!" he pleaded. "Do you want to get us evicted?"

The turret door stood open; the staircase rose like a piece of sculpture; the windows sparkled. Some old furniture was jammed into the room—odd bedroom pieces with cracked mirrors. Apparently no one knew it was there when the Limburger furnishings were liquidated.

Two inquisitive cats entered the turret room cautiously, but instead of running up the spiral staircase and peering out the windows, they preferred to sniff the furniture.

"Cats!" Qwilleran said aloud. "Who can outguess them?"

Koko was trying to open a dresser drawer. Yum Yum was investigating another cat in a cracked mirror.

Only old friends can be invited to dinner at the last minute, and the Rikers were friends of long standing, and no minute was ever too late for a dinner invitation. Arch Riker, now the publisher of the *Moose County Something,* had grown up with Qwilleran in Chicago. Mildred Riker, a native of Moose County and now food editor for the paper, had the kind of comfortable, outgoing personality that made new friends feel like old friends.

On this occasion Qwilleran had hinted at a fantastic discovery that would make big news; the Rikers reported to the inn at six o'clock sharp. "Welcome to the Nutcracker Inn," he greeted them.

"They should have called it the Squirrel House," Arch said.

Nevertheless he was mightily impressed by the black walnut woodwork. Mildred raved about the coral tint of walls and tablecloths that made everyone look good. Both were surprised to hear that the rich texture of the painted walls was accomplished by grinding up black walnut shells and adding them to the paint.

They were seated at a table in the front window where they could enjoy the June evening and the comic cavorting of squirrels. Mildred said, "It doesn't seem right to be here without Polly. Have you heard from her, Qwill?"

"She left only yesterday. Her sister is flying from Cincinnati and meeting her in Virginia."

"Have you ever met her sister?" Arch asked.

Playfully Qwilleran replied, "No, and sometimes I wonder if Polly really has a sister in Cincinnati."

"She might have another man in Cincinnati," Arch suggested.

"Shame on you both," Mildred rebuked them. "You were naughty schoolboys, and now you're naughty men!"

The two men exchanged mischievous glances and Arch said with glee, "In fourth grade Qwill composed disrespectful couplets about our teachers. I remember: *'Old Miss Perkins, flat as a pie, never had a boyfriend, and we know why.'* "

"Not one of my better couplets," Qwilleran admitted. "Arch peddled them around the school yard for a penny apiece and that's where we made our mistake— going commercial."

Arch ordered a martini and suggested consulting the menu. "There's a documentary on TV that I want to see tonight."

Qwilleran asked, "Any hot news from the big city, Arch? I've been gone since eight o'clock this morning."

"Well!" Mildred announced with authority. "Fran Brodie was seen having dinner with Dr. Prelligate at the Palomino Paddock. They were drinking champagne! Everyone's wondering if they're serious."

"Serious about what?" her husband asked. "I'm serious about having my dinner."

The salads were served, and Mildred began her editorial of the evening. "Historically, salads were intended to refresh the palate before the rich dessert. Restaurants started serving them first to keep customers busy and happy while waiting for the steak. Mothers started serving them first because kids and husbands hated salads but would eat them at the beginning of the meal when they were ravenously hungry."

"I'm with the husbands," Qwilleran said. "I hate salads."

"The sour taste of most dressings is too sophisticated for many palates. When my daughter was a teen, she used to put sugar on the French dressing."

"Yuk!" said her husband.

"Please pass the sugar," Qwilleran said.

All three diners ordered the same thing and agreed that the leg of lamb was superb but the strawberry pie wasn't as good as Mildred's. There was no lingering over coffee; the Rikers wanted to see the unique staircase.

Koko and Yum Yum met them at the door of 3-FF and followed them to the turret room.

"Fantastic! A work of art," Mildred cried. "And over a hundred years old!"

Arch said, "We could use a three-column shot of this on the front page Monday. . . . Okay if we send a photographer tomorrow? He'll call first. . . . It'll be picked up by papers around the state and even TV. . . . But this furniture will have to be moved out of the way."

"It's all black walnut!" Mildred cried. "And that low chest is a dower chest! It has the bride's name on it!"

Lettered on the front of it, in fancy script, was "Elsa Limburger." "Oh, let's look inside!"

It was indeed filled with wedding finery, lace-trimmed and embroidered, but dreary with age.

"How sad! The poor girl died before her wedding," Mildred went on. "Her parents were so distraught, they couldn't bear to look at the furniture she would have taken into her new home."

Qwilleran knew otherwise, but he allowed his friend to have her romantic fantasy. As for the cracked mirrors, he had a theory. On the dressing table, bureau and cheval glass there were spidery cracks radiating from a central hole. He could imagine Elsa's enraged father going from mirror to mirror and smashing it with the signet ring on his fist. It would be a large, ostentatious chunk of gold.

Then the Rikers had to leave, and on the way to the elevator Arch asked Qwilleran if he would like to review the play opening Friday night at the high school auditorium. He said, "The Mooseland Choral Society is doing it, and they're supposed to be very good. And since you're living here . . ."

"No thanks," said Qwilleran.

"You wouldn't have to file your copy until Monday morning."

"No thanks."

"It's *Pirates of Penzance* and you like Gilbert and Sullivan."

"No thanks."

After his guests had gone home to their TV documentary, Qwilleran had a thought about the "dark cloud" that Lori sensed in the building. He was not superstitious, but if one wanted to make a case, three broken mirrors in the basement should be as unlucky as three on the third floor. The furniture should be removed from the premises! He phoned the office. "Nick, can you stand some good news?"

"Don't tell me. Let me guess. Koko won the lottery."

"Better than that! The *Something* wants to run the turret staircase on page one. It's the kind of curiosity the media will pick up around the state. But we have to move the furniture out in a hurry."

"We can stack it in the basement."

Qwilleran thought fast: If Lori's "dark cloud" theory were true, having the three broken mirrors in the basement wouldn't help much. He said, "Well, here's the situation, Nick. The stuff is very valuable, and it's the property of the K Fund, actually. We should move it to a storage unit on Sandpit Road. The K Fund will cover the rental."

Nick was always agreeable. "Sure thing! Keith is on duty tonight. He and I can do it. I think the facility is open all night."

"I'll go along," Qwilleran said. "Maybe I can help."

The Siamese had to be sequestered in the bedroom again as the black walnut treasures were being moved to the elevator, and Qwilleran wondered, Why were they more interested in the furniture than the staircase? There was a reason, but one would have to be a cat to know the answer.

chapter three

Before going in to breakfast Sunday morning, Qwilleran visited the small boutique in the office. It sold postcards of the inn, small bags of peanuts for the squirrels, insect repellent, and the official Moose County T-shirt in sizes small to ex- tra-extra large. Across the front of the shirt was splashed a moose head fifteen inches wide. Nature had given the animal a dour expression that was comic or ugly, de- pending on one's sense of humor, and Qwilleran wanted to buy one for Arch Riker.

The two men enjoyed playing tricks on each other, much as they had done when they were eight years old. Riker wrote ab- surd fan letters, anonymously, to the "Qwill Pen" columnist who, in turn, sent unsuitable gifts, anonymously, to the editor and publisher.

As for the famous black walnut staircase, it had already been photographed by Roger MacGillivray, former history teacher now working for the *Something.* Qwilleran knew him to be an ailurophobe and had locked the Siamese in the bedroom before Roger's arrival.

"Where are they?" the pale young man asked.

"In the bedroom, handcuffed to the bedpost, and—in case they get loose and break down the bedroom door—they're muzzled!"

The photographer exposed plenty of film, showing the staircase from all angles. In one of them a bushy-tailed squirrel could be seen peering through the window. "That's it! That's the one they'll use!"

"Can you join me for breakfast, Rog?"

"I'd like to, but I'm the only leg man on duty, and I've gotta shoot a couple of paintings at the art center—best-of-show and popular favorite. I don't know what to expect. They're self-portraits by kids."

"I was one of the judges," said Qwilleran,

"and I can tell you right now that the winner won't reproduce in black-and-white. It's a girl with pale yellow hair and pale blue eyes, wearing a pale pink dress against a pale lavender background."

"All I can do is print it up as contrasty as possible—and explain to the picture desk. Maybe they can cover it in the cutline."

The Siamese were beginning to howl, and Roger made a quick exit.

In the dining room Qwilleran was seated at a table next to a couple involved in animated discussion. They were dressed as if they had just come from church. They were fortyish and spirited enough to make Qwilleran wonder who they were. He opened the *Wilson Quarterly* he had brought along and pretended to read while listening. The man was husky and had a firm jaw, twinkling eyes, and a tuft of hair falling boyishly over his forehead; the woman had a pleasant voice and expressive hands.

The man asked, "So it's definite that he's going to come and speak?"

"Oh, yes! We're covering all his expenses. The date will be firmed up tomorrow. We're quite flexible on that score."

"Who will attend?"

"Only MCCC people."

"Do you know the gist of his speech?"

"The future of MCCC: opportunities, problems, warnings. It should be the most important event we've ever had."

"It certainly seems so."

They ordered chicken liver omelets; Qwilleran had eggs Benedict. Both finished at about the same time. They paid by credit card and left the dining room. Qwilleran charged his brunch to 3FF and followed them into the lobby, where the man was looking at a photo exhibit of ancient black walnut trees with enormous trunks.

The hostess said, "Mr. Qwilleran, did you enjoy your brunch?"

The man with the firm jaw and twinkling eyes whirled around. "Mr. Qwilleran! My wife and I are avid readers of yours! I'm Bruce Abernethy."

"And compliments to you, doctor, on your letter to the editor Friday."

"Someone has to speak up," was the

modest reply. "This is my wife, Nell. She keeps a 'Qwill Pen' scrapbook."

Merrily she said, "He passed up a Henrietta and a Thomasina to get a one-syllable wife."

"It wasn't her name I went for; it was her black walnut pie."

"Mr. Q, if we promise to serve it at the MCCC luncheon, will you be our guest of honor?"

"It would be my pleasure!" He was quite sincere. He had been looking for an appropriate entrée into the hard-shelled academic clique at the college.

"Wonderful! We're having a guest speaker, but I'll have to notify you of the time and place."

Then the doctor said, "Andrew Brodie told us you were spending a few weeks in Black Creek—and that you might be interested in an experience I had at the age of eleven."

"Yow-w-w!" came an unearthly sound from the upper floors. Everyone in the lobby looked up.

"I would!!" Qwilleran said with a distracted glance upstairs.

"Yow-w-w!"

"That's my cat! Excuse me . . ."

"Call me! Wednesday's my day off!"

Qwilleran ran up the stairs three at a time, and even as he unlocked the door to 3FF, the tumult increased.

"Please!" he scolded Koko. "This is a public establishment! If you don't moderate your crescendos, they'll kick us out!"

It was a weak argument, because that was probably what the crafty rogue wanted.

Qwilleran tried a different tack. "How would you like a walk down to the creek?" He dangled the harness and leash, causing Yum Yum to disappear and Koko to prowl in anticipation.

"Going for a walk" meant that the man walked and the cat rode on his shoulder, securely harnessed and leashed. They rode the elevator and went out the back door to avoid inquisitive guests in the lobby. When they started downhill to the creek, however, well-meaning sightseers converged on them with the usual naïve comments and gender confusion.

"Is that a *cat*?"

"It's so skinny!"

"Hey, look! She has blue eyes!"

"Does he bite?"

"Nice kitty! Nice kitty!"

"Is it a girl or a boy?"

Kao K'o Kung—from his lofty perch— looked down on the rabble in disdain. As for Qwilleran, he had some snippy replies to their questions, but he held his tongue. Squirrels scattered at the sight of the cat, each running up its favorite tree. One of them had her baby tucked under her chin, while its tiny forelegs clutched her neck.

At the water's edge seven crows strutted nonchalantly. Trout jumped out of the water for skeeters, causing Koko to jerk his head excitedly, this way and that. Then his body stiffened; Qwilleran could feel the tension on his shoulder. Did the cat see an otter swimming, or a raccoon on the opposite shore? No, something was drifting down the creek.

Qwilleran glanced in several directions before dashing toward the first cabin. "Do you have a phone?" he shouted to someone on the screened porch. "I need to call

911!" He was now clutching a struggling cat under one arm.

A woman let him in and pointed indoors. "On the kitchen wall!" She turned off some music.

To the operator he said, "There's a body floating downstream in the Black Creek. It just passed the Nutcracker Inn, about half a mile south of the Stone Bridge—moving slowly—not much current. Face down— fully clothed—I think it's a man."

"Oh, dear!" the woman said when he hung up. "I couldn't help hearing what you said. Isn't that awful! Must have fallen out of a boat." She clutched her throat, and her face flushed. "It's so upsetting—a drowning . . ."

"Sit down, ma'am. I'll get you a glass of water," said Qwilleran, still clutching Koko, looped with a few feet of leash and squirming irritably. "Try to relax, ma'am. Take some slow deep breaths."

She sipped the water gratefully, nodding her thanks. "My husband drowned . . . four years ago."

"I know how you must feel. A terrible tragedy! But don't try to talk yet. Do you

mind if I put the cat down on the floor?"
She waved an assent; he released the
struggling animal while keeping a firm
hand on the leash.

"Thank you so much," she said with a
deep sigh. "He was a commercial fisherman . . . a sudden storm . . . left three
families of widows and orphans."

Koko was now prowling in a zigzag,
nose to the floor like a bloodhound. While
keeping an eye on him Qwilleran said, "I
remember the incident. I knew those men.
I'd been out on the lake with the commercial fleet—"

"You're Mr. Q. I recognized you from
your picture in the paper. You wrote a
beautiful story—"

"Are you a Hawley or a Scotten?"

"Hannah Hawley."

Koko had found the built-in dinette and
was standing on a bench with forelegs on
the table, while sniffing left and right.

"Koko!"

The stern reprimand was unheeded. He
went on sniffing.

"He smells my glue," said Mrs. Hawley

with some amusement. "He can't hurt anything."

"Glue?" The cat had a passion for adhesives and could smell a postage stamp across the room.

"I make miniature furnishings for doll houses."

"You do?" He stroked his moustache as his mental computer recognized an idea for the "Qwill Pen." "I'd like to talk to you about your craft. Perhaps you'd have dinner with me at the inn tonight."

"I'd love to!"

"I'll call for you at six o'clock," Qwilleran said as he coaxed Koko away from the glue pot.

He waited for Lori to be alone in her office and then went in to say, "Have you heard the good news?"

"We're going to be on the front page!" she cried. "I'm thrilled!"

"They wanted the old furniture out of the way, so it was moved to Sandpit Road in the middle of the night as Nick probably told you. And do you know what, Lori? I believe we've discovered the source of the bad vibes you were getting! According to the history of the place, those particular items of furniture were connected with the family tragedy."

"I knew it!" she cried. "There was a negative influence at work, but this morning the pall has been lifted!"

"I feel euphoric myself," Qwilleran said, to be agreeable. Actually, he attributed it to the eggs Benedict.

"Do you find your suite comfortable, Qwill?"

"I have no complaint, but I'm afraid Koko's yowling will annoy lodgers on the second floor. He can even be heard in the lobby. A cabin would be more suitable—with its screened porch, windows on four sides, and proximity to the water and wildlife. Will there be a vacancy soon? Otherwise, we may have to return to Pickax."

"I understand," she said.

"They're accustomed to a huge barn with three balconies and overhead beams and rafters. It isn't fair to coop them up like this. They're all the family I've got, and I have to consider their welfare." His impassioned plea was not solely altruistic. He, too, would prefer a cabin and the idea of taking meals at the inn for two weeks appealed mightily.

Fingering the guest register, she said, "Mr. Hackett is supposed to check out of cabin number five today, but he hasn't returned his key. His car is gone, and when the housekeeper went down there to check, she found his luggage half packed. He may have gone to church, and someone invited him home to dinner."

"Ye-e-ess," Qwilleran said doubtfully, and he patted his moustache. "Who is he? Do you know?"

"A business traveler. The name of his company sounds like building supplies. We have his credit card number and can't turn him out if he wishes to stay. He really should let us know his plans."

"Meanwhile," Qwilleran said, "I'll state the case to the guys upstairs and entreat their cooperation."

On the way, he stepped into the library. During the Limburgers' residence the shelves had been filled with gold-tooled, leather-bound volumes, probably unread. Now there were mellow old books that guests might enjoy reading: *Gone with the Wind* and *Wuthering Heights,* and titles of that sort. Qwilleran borrowed a collection of Hans Christian Andersen's fairy tales to read to the Siamese and keep them quiet.

It worked! They listened in fascination as he read the story of the ugly duckling that grew up to be a beautiful swan. There were plenty of animals in the tale, and Qwilleran had a talent for impersonating the peeping duckling, his quacking mother, clucking hen, meowing cats, cawing ravens, and so forth. It was ironic that the beautiful swans communicated with hair-raising screeches! Exhausted by the excitement of it all, Koko and Yum Yum crept away for their naps.

Just as Qwilleran was congratulating himself, he received a phone call from Lori. "Qwill, is everything all right up there?"

"Everything's fine! I've been reading to the cats, and I believe it calmed them down."

"That's strange. We had a phone call

from a guest, saying that something terrible was happening in 3FF."

"Someone must be watching television," he said.

When the time came for dinner with Mrs. Hawley, Qwilleran walked down the hill with a tape recorder in his pocket. On the way he watched for mother squirrels carrying their babies, but all he saw was father squirrels chasing mother squirrels.

Hannah was waiting for him on the porch, gaily clad in a blouse printed with oversized hibiscus blossoms. She was an expert at makeup and looked quite attractive.

"Where do you spend your winters?" he asked as they started to walk up the hill. He knew the answer.

"In Florida," she said. "My daughter runs a restaurant on the Gulf Coast, and I give her a hand. But this is where I belong. All my relatives and friends are here. The Scotten and Hawley families."

"The fishocracy of Moose County," he

said. "Is Doris still selling home-baked goods?"

"Yes, but Magnus is getting ready to retire. She's my sister-in-law."

"And Aubrey. Is he still keeping bees?"

"He's my nephew."

"I knew him when he was taking care of old Gus Limburger, and I admired his patience with the old curmudgeon."

"Gus had a cuckoo clock in the entrance hall, and he promised to leave it to Bree, but he never got it. Someone around here must have taken it when Gus died."

Qwilleran made a mental note to find out what happened to Aubrey's cuckoo clock. "Since I know your whole family, I'm going to call you Hannah, and you must call me Qwill. I take it, you're here for the entire summer. Do you know the people in the other cabins?"

"Only Wendy and Doyle Underhill in the middle cabin. Nice young couple. Both teachers. She's writing a family history. He goes around photographing wildlife."

"There's a small boy in the cabin next to you."

"Yes. Poor Danny. He has no one to play

with, and his parents don't seem to give him any attention. I took a plate of cookies over there and introduced myself. Danny's mother said she's recuperating after surgery, and her husband spends his time deep-sea fishing on the charter boats. I think she watches a lot of TV. I asked if my singing bothered her, and she said no."

After they had been seated in the dining room, and after they had ordered from the menu, Qwilleran placed his tape recorder on the table. "Mind if I tape this interview?"

"Are you really going to write about my hobby?"

"If you give intelligent answers to my dumb questions. For starters, what attracted you to doll houses?"

"Well, my mother let me fix up my own room when I was in high school, and I secretly took a correspondence course in home decorating. I was in my early twenties when I married Jeb, and I went to work on the old Scotten house we got for a wedding present. It was so plain and so gloomy! I painted and wallpapered and slip covered and made curtains, and that's where we raised our family."

"What did Jeb think about your efforts?"

"Oh, he was very proud of me!" She bit her lip. "After he drowned, I sold the house and went to Florida to be with my daughter. And that's where I discovered this doll house store! They sold miniature furnishings and equipment for do-it-yourselfers! That was me! I learned all about paint and glue and handling fabrics and cutting moldings."

"Did you find it difficult to think small?" Qwilleran asked.

"Not really. On a one-to-twelve scale, one inch equals one foot. You can paint a whole room with half a cup of paint."

"And a very small brush, I imagine. . . . Where did you start? What was your first project?"

"An old-fashioned dining room. I bought the table, six chairs, a sideboard, a mantelpiece and a gaslight style of chandelier. I stained the furniture, rubbed it with ash to look old, stenciled the walls to look like wallpaper, upholstered the chair seats, and so forth. For a rug I daubed designs on a nine-by-twelve-inch piece of velvet."

"How long did this take?"

"You don't count the hours when you're having fun, Qwill, or solving a problem or developing an idea. My miniature dining room needed candlesticks, a table center-piece and pictures to hang on the walls. Using a small miter box to cut moldings with clean corners, I made the frames for thumbnail-size pictures. One was a por-trait of a blue jay—actually a postage stamp."

"What's the smallest detail that ever con-fronted you?"

She had to think a while. "Well, in my country kitchen I had a one-inch cat curled up asleep on the hearth, with some food left in his half-inch bowl, and a mouse was sneaking up to steal some of it. The prob-lem was, what to use for the tail of a mouse that's only a sixth of an inch long."

"Dare I ask what you decided to use?"

She looked smug. "A bristle from my toothbrush! Of course, it had to be painted mouse-gray."

As he escorted her back to her cabin, Qwilleran asked, "Do you have a finished project that I could see?"

"I'm afraid I've given them all to friends and relatives, but they've all been photographed, and I could show you some eight-by-tens. Shall we sit on the porch and have a glass of lemonade?"

Hannah's miniature rooms were incredible, and the photography was excellent. "Who shot these?" Qwilleran asked.

"John Bushland."

"I know Bushy. He's the best in the county."

"He does it as a courtesy," she explained. "His family used to be in commercial fishing."

As Hannah related the baffling story about the disappearance of the Bushland boat and crew, which he had heard before, Qwilleran laid his plans: He would run the interview in his Tuesday column . . . and get Junior Goodwinter to devote the Tuesday picture page to six miniature rooms . . . using Bushy's photos.

She interrupted his concentration with a

question. "Do you like Gilbert and Sulli-
van? The Mooseland chorus is presenting
Pirates of Penzance next weekend, and
I'm singing the role of Ruth the nursemaid.
If you're interested, I can get you tickets."

"Thank you," he said, "but as a matter of
fact, I'm reviewing it for the newspaper."

On returning to the inn, he found
Nick in the office. "Has Koko been
disturbing the peace?"

"Nope. All quiet on the third-floor front."

"Any word from the guy in the end
cabin?"

"Nope. I'm going down to scout the
scene. Want to come?"

"May I bring Koko? Any little diversion
will improve his disposition."

They drove down the hill and parked behind Cabin Five. Nick used his master key,
and the three of them entered specula-
tively: Koko sniffing everything, Qwilleran
appraising the accommodations, Nick
scanning the premises for clues to Hackett's intentions. His luggage was half
packed, and gray trousers, white polo shirt

and brown oxfords were laid out for the trip. In the bathroom the contents of a toiletries kit were scattered about: toothbrush, dentifrice, denture bath, shaving needs, foot powder, analgesic muscle rub, and so forth.

Nick checked the plumbing, refrigerator, TV and lamps. "As soon as we can get rid of him, Qwill, the housekeeper will make up the room, and you can move in."

Koko was inordinately curious about the oxfords. Qwilleran thought, It's the foot powder; the cat was suspicious of anything with a medicinal odor. Then he went into the bathroom and found a green plastic box with a hinged lid—the denture bath. Qwilleran thought, He thinks he's found a treasure. "It makes him feel important," he explained.

"Well, nothing more we can do," Nick said. "Let's go."

He was locking the back door when a loud, angry voice came from the next cabin. He said, "That's Mrs. Truffle laying out the contractor who's building her house, or her attorney in Milwaukee, or her nephew in Detroit. Judging from the rocks she wears, she's loaded, and she likes to throw her weight around. . . . It's time for the nightly news. Shall we turn on the car radio?"

They heard the WPKX announcer say, "The body of an adult male was found in the Black Creek north of the Stone Bridge earlier today—fully clothed but without identification. The victim was described as about forty, six feet tall, weighing about one-seventy, and having dark hair, upper and lower dentures, and a prominent birthmark under the left ear. If this description fits anyone thought to be missing, listeners are urged to notify the sheriff.

"It's him!" Nick shouted. "I remember the birthmark."

Qwilleran looked at Koko and remembered the denture bath.

chapter four

As Qwilleran was shaving on Monday morning, he noticed the cats watching the door to the hall. Yum Yum's tail was waving amiably while Koko's was bushed, and a growl deep in his chest rose to a snarl in high C.

Qwilleran opened the door a quarter of an inch and closed it quickly. He went to the phone and called the office.

Lori answered cheerfully, "Good morning! Nutcracker Inn." She was a different person, now that the three broken mirrors were gone. Or so it seemed. He was not prepared to believe it.

Gruffly he said, "We are being held hostage in suite 3FF! Would you call off your rodent control officer?"

"Oh, Qwill! Is Nicodemus up there? I'll send the porter for him. Perhaps we should confine him to our cottage until you move into your cabin."

"What's the situation down by the creek? Did Nick call the sheriff last night?"

"Yes, and he had to go to Pickax to iden- tify the body! He didn't get home until three this morning! I'm letting him sleep in. The drowned man is our Mr. Hackett, all right, but we can't rent the cabin until the state police detectives inspect it. That's all I know, but it sounds suspicious, doesn't it? Nick can give you the details. I'll have him call you when he wakes up."

When Qwilleran went downstairs to breakfast, he vetoed the quiche that the server was promoting and or- dered ham and eggs with American fries. There were times when only comfort food would do. He reveled in the familiar old tastes and textures, at the same time reviewing his evening with Hannah Hawley. It had been a pleasant occasion as well as a productive interview. And when he confessed that he had sung the role of the pirate king during his college days, she was not surprised; she could identify a fine voice quality when she heard one.

She said, "Why don't you join the Mooseland chorus, Qwill? It's a wonderful feeling—singing together and being in harmony with others. And you'd like Uncle Louie, our director. He makes every rehearsal *fun!* He's from Canada and knows Gilbert and Sullivan backward and forward."

And then Qwilleran had said, "If I couldn't be Shakespeare, I'd like to be W. S. Gilbert, composing farcical plots and outrageous lyrics."

Together they made a list of favorite rhymes: *man's affection* and *bad complexion . . . matters mathematical* and *simple and quadratical . . . A lot of news* and *hypotenuse . . . Felonious little crimes* and *merry village chimes.*

Hannah had trained as a music teacher. "But then, Jeb came along," she said with a sigh. "If he were living now, he'd be so proud to have me written up in the 'Qwill Pen' column!"

After breakfast, fortified by three cups of coffee, Qwilleran went upstairs and gave the Siamese a morsel of ham he had sneaked out of the dining room. Then he wrote a thousand words about the doll house miniatures that he could not honestly appreciate, although he admired the skill, patience, and creativity that went into them. He also phoned Junior Goodwinter, to save a three-column horizontal hole for a photo on page two. It was an old-fashioned bedroom with fireplace, four-poster bed, and rugs braided of knitting yarn. The wash stand was equipped with one-inch towels and a tiny bowl-and-pitcher set and even tinier soap dish. The cake of soap was an aspirin tablet.

While waiting for Nick's phone call, Qwilleran played the video of *Pirates* that Hannah had lent him—to refresh his memory about plot, characters and dialogue. The Siamese went to the turret to watch squirrels; there were no birds or animals on the TV screen.

Qwilleran turned it off and hurried downstairs to hear the latest.

"Well, the sheriff's office wanted me to rush to the morgue and identify the body. I also took the guest register, but who knows if the information is true. I remembered that Hackett had worn a big digital wristwatch; that's all I could contribute. I know the fellows in the sheriff's department very well and wanted to ask a few questions, but the state detectives were there. You press guys are the only ones that can ask questions and get away with it."

"That doesn't say we get answers."

"Maybe the paper will have an update. It's delivered here at two-thirty. I suppose you noticed the police cars coming and going to the cabin, Qwill. They've got it taped off."

"Probably brushing for fingerprints. They'll pick up some of Koko's nose prints."

Nick asked, "How are the cats?"

"Calmed down since yesterday—until Nicodemus paid a social call this morning."

"Don't worry. He'll stay in our cottage until you move to the cabin."

Qwilleran had some time to kill before dining with Barb Ogilvie, and he walked aimlessly about the grounds.

Once he stopped to watch a squirrel frantically digging a hole. It was so deep that his foreleg disappeared in the excavation as each teaspoonful of soil was brought to the surface. Then he buried some small treasure, scooping the earth back into the hole, tamping it with a paw, and camouflaging the site with fallen leaves.

Qwilleran's built-in "Qwill Pen" alarm system signaled a topic for Friday's column: Squirrels! Everyone loves them or hates them!

It would be possible to do man-on-the-street interviews without even leaving the inn! It was the kind of column that would virtually write itself! The reader response would pour into the newspaper office, making Arch Riker happy!

Perfect!

Meanwhile there was action in the lobby of the inn. The personable young MCCC student who was Lori's part-time apprentice was arranging an exhibit in the glass display case that kept guests entertained while waiting for tables in the dining room.

The previous exhibit had been a collection of photos showing the Limburger mansion, inside and out, before it was renovated by the Klingenschoen Fund. Outside, there were broken bricks, boarded up windows, overgrown weeds—and squirrels. Inside, there were dark walls, ponderous items of furniture shipped from Germany, a cuckoo clock, and cartons of rubbish. The photos were augmented by a few items of German porcelain and wood-carving, salvaged from the clutter when everything else was unloaded.

Now the enthusiastic apprentice, whose name was Cathy, was arranging a collection of vintage nutcrackers. A computer-printed sign said BLACK WALNUTS ARE A HARD NUT TO CRACK.

"Nice job, Cathy," said Qwilleran. "If you

don't make it as president of an interna-
tional hotel chain, you can always get a
job as a window-trimmer."

"You say such nice things, Mr. Q!"

"Where did you get the artifacts?"

"Dr. Abernethy is lending them."

"Can the case be locked?" Qwilleran
was thinking of the cuckoo clock that had
been spirited out of the building before the
renovation, although it had been promised
to Aubrey Scotten. He was a young man
who gave much and asked for little. He
should have received the clock promised
him.

When the bundle of Monday papers arrived in the lobby, everyone grabbed.
There on the front page was the black walnut staircase, with a squirrel peering in the
window. She probably had a nest between
the turret and the mansard roof. It was
photographer's luck that she happened to
be there at the right moment.

In the News Bite column, the unidentified body found in Black Creek was still
unidentified, although the victim was not a
local resident, it had been determined. In

other words, he was an outsider, using an alias.

Coverage of the third-grade portrait exhibit was extensive. As Qwilleran had predicted, the pale-tinted best-of-show reproduced poorly, but the copy desk had handled it well. The cutline read: "Color my hair yellow. Color my eyes blue. Color my dress pink. Or visit the art center before June 30 and see for yourself why Lisa LaPorte's pastel won best of show."

As for the popular vote, it went to a youngster named Robb Campbell. His self-portrait had scarecrow hair, jug ears, and a wide grin with one front tooth missing.

Qwilleran waited until five o'clock, when legmen on the news beat would be reporting to their departments. Then he phoned the photo lab and congratulated Roger on the excellence of his staircase photo and the size of his byline.

"Yeah . . . well . . . the squirrel deserves most of the credit."

"I hear there was some excitement on the police beat. Any further news?"

"Uh . . . Can't talk now, Qwill. Got prints coming through."

"See you later." To Qwilleran, Roger's "uh . . ." meant that he had the story-behind-the-story. He would call Roger at home, after dinner with Barb Ogilvie.

At six o'clock he waited for his guest to drive into the parking lot and then went out to meet her.

"You're so gallant!" she said. "You're a vanishing breed!"

"I'd rather be an endangered species," he said. "It doesn't sound terminal. . . . You're looking spiffy, Barb." She was wearing bright red, and he wondered how it would look with the pale coral walls and tablecloths.

Heads turned as they were ushered to a table. Some would be wondering, Where's Polly?

She said, "This is the first time I've seen the inn. Fran did a good job. I'd love to see the carved staircase that was in today's paper."

"It's in a private suite—and not on view. . . . What are you drinking tonight?"

She asked for a margarita—not a popular cocktail in Moose County.

He said, "It seems to me that you had a sizable rock on your ring finger, the last time I saw you."

"That's ancient history!"

"Too bad. Everyone thought you and Barry Morghan were a perfect couple."

"I was perfect for him, but he wasn't perfect for me!"

"Would any man be perfect for you?" Her attachments were known to be short-lived.

"You would!" she replied flippantly, rolling her eyes.

"Strike that last question," he said. "Shall we consult the menu?"

She ordered pork loin with quince and cinnamon glaze and then played it safe by talking business. "The coverage of our exhibit was great! And attendance was excellent. We thought friends and relatives would vote for their own third-grader, but they surprised us. They loved that caricature with a tooth missing. The artist was

Robb Campbell, and when I met him, I was shocked! He was neatly combed and had flat ears and all his teeth!"

"An opportunist," Qwilleran said. "He'll go far—but not necessarily in the right direction."

"I asked him why he played such a trick, and he said, 'That's how I feel inside.' How do you like that, Qwill?"

"I'm not sure I know. Kids have changed a lot since I was eight."

"Well, anyway, the good news is that people who have never been to the art center came to see this kid show. Maybe they'll come again, attend a lecture, take a class."

Qwilleran recommended a glass of pink zinfandel with her entrée and then asked, "How's everything in the world of wool? Are you still knitting? Is your mother still spinning? Is your father still shearing sheep? Is Duncan still herding the flock?"

"Oh, let me tell you what my knitting club is doing! We're knitting knee-high socks for the pirates in *Pirates of Penzance* to wear with black breeches—wide stripes of red, black and white! We think they'll catch on with the tourists, too. They can be worn with shorts, you know. . . . Would you like a pair, Qwill?"

"I think not. They'd scare the cats." He could visualize the streets of Mooseville, swarming with tourists in moose head T-shirts, baggy shorts and pirate socks— and smelling of anti-skeeter spray.

Dinner with Barb Ogilvie was always lively, but toward the end Qwilleran was eager to go upstairs and phone Roger at home.

The photographer was quick to pick up the phone. "Hey, Qwill! Glad you called. Sorry I couldn't talk downtown, but you know how it is."

"I understand perfectly. Let me tell you why I called. I have a vested interest in the case. The victim was in the process of vacating a cabin I'm supposed to rent, but now the police have it sealed. Do I move back to Pickax? Or what? Any crumb of information that will help me make a decision . . ."

"I know what you mean. Wait'll I close the door." A door slammed. "First off, it's definitely a homicide, but they're calling it

an accident so the suspect won't go fugitive."

"Cause of death?"

"Blow to the head."

"Well, thanks. It isn't much, but it helps."

So, Qwilleran asked himself, had
someone wanted Hackett's forty-
thousand-dollar car badly enough to kill
for it? Or was there another motive? That
being the case, where did the attack take
place? And what was Hackett doing there
early on a Sunday morning? And how did
he end up in the creek, upstream from the
Nutcracker?

The creek came down through a dense
forest owned by the Klingenschoen Foundation and known as the Black Forest
Conservancy. Qwilleran stroked his moustache. He was getting a familiar sensation
on his upper lip.

chapter five

On Tuesday morning, Qwilleran gave the Siamese a fine breakfast, some intelligent conversation and ten minutes of sport with the old necktie. Even so, they regarded him reproachfully, huddled in a compact bundle of fur, fluffed up to show disapproval.

"I'm sorry, you guys," he said. "I'm doing the best I can. As soon as the police release the cabin, we'll move. Bear with me!" They merely sulked.

At least they're not raising the roof, he thought.

He was taking the copy for Tuesday's "Qwill Pen" to be faxed in the manager's office. When he arrived, Lori was on the phone, however, and he waited in the hall. She was saying:

"Yes, I know . . . I know, Mrs. Truffle,

but . . . I agree, it was most unfortunate, but . . . Mrs. Truffle, will you let me explain that our insurance will cover repairs . . . On the contrary, they do expert repairs, but it will mean sending it to Chicago. When are you leaving for Milwaukee? . . . And when will you return? . . . Then we'll wait till you get back, and you can supervise the shipping . . . No! No! You have nothing to worry about. The repairs will be undetectable . . . Hope you have a nice—" Lori was interrupted by a slammed receiver.

"Excuse me," Qwilleran said. "Are you having trouble?"

"Sit down, Qwill. That was Mrs. Truffle, who is renting one of the cabins while a local contractor is building a vacation home for her. She's going to Milwaukee on business for a couple of days. The last time she went, squirrels gnawed through the roof and chewed one of the Oriental rugs she'd brought up for the new house. They also dragged some of her underwear through the hole in the roof—good nesting material, I suppose."

Qwilleran chuckled. "She sounds like the kind of person who attracts glitches."

"They never told me that innkeeping would be like this . . . What can I do for you, Qwill? Is that your copy for today's paper? I'll fax it right away."

Going into the dining room for breakfast, he took a table near a couple who were mesmerized by the squirrel show outside the window.

"They're fantastic," said the woman.

"They're rodents!" said the man.

"Well, I think they're adorable. Beautiful tails!"

"They're rodents!"

Leaving the dining room without a second cup of coffee, he came upon Nick Bamba, going to the post office for mail. "Want to ride along, Qwill?"

As they drove away from the inn, Qwilleran said, "I'm going to write my next column on squirrels."

"The price of peanuts will go up all over the county," the innkeeper said cynically.

"I hope you don't mind if I poll your

lodgers. Not everyone will be pro-squirrel."

"That's all right. I'm not a hundred percent in favor of the hungry horde myself. I know they're a big attraction but they multiply exponentially, and next year we'll be wading shin-deep in fluffy tails."

Qwilleran chuckled. "When the Klingenschoen Foundation bought the mansion for an inn, they thought the squirrels were an asset."

"What do those guys in Chicago know?"

He began his public opinion poll on the patio at the rear of the inn, where guests gathered to watch the performers' acrobatics . . . and to simper over the friendliness of the hungry little animals. The tape recorder in his pocket captured it all:

"Look! He's not afraid of me! He comes right up to me for a peanut!"

"Be careful, Stella. They have sharp teeth."

"It's wonderful—don't you think?—that a wild animal is so trusting of humans?"

"Their tails are so graceful!"

"They have such bright, intelligent eyes!"

"And great ingenuity. Did you ever see one get at a squirrel-proof birdfeeder? He studies it for a while and then figures it out."

"I had to stop feeding birds. I was filling the feeder three times a day. We'd rather have the squirrels."

"We'd rather have the birds."

"Well, that's what makes horse racing, isn't it?"

(Laughter.)

"It's not always funny. Our whole town was blacked out for thirty hours when a squirrel gnawed an overhead power line."

"What happened to the squirrel?"

(Laughter.)

"The window-washer told me there's a nest on the roof, between the turret and the slate—just like the crook of a tree. That's him running up and down the side of the building."

"It's not a *him;* it's a *her.* She goes up to feed her babies."

From the patio Qwilleran went into the conservatory, where some of the older guests were watching the squirrels through the glass.

"My sister-in-law was in a deep depression, but the daily visits of a gray squirrel got her out of it."

"Squirrels are God's gifts to humans. I never let anyone say anything against them."

"They have a lot of squirrels in Washington—"

"You can say that again! Ha ha ha!"

"One year they planted five thousand dollars' worth of bulbs in the White House flower beds, and the squirrels dug them all up."

"I'll bet somebody made political hay out of that little mistake!"

"I'll bet they had a Squirrelgate Investigation! Ha ha ha!"

"Our dog chases them up a tree, and they turn around and laugh at him. Drives him berserk!"

"They're born comedians!"

"They're rodents! If they didn't have those bushy tails, there'd be a law against them."

"One winter we went to Florida and

squirrels got into our attic and had a ball! They like attics."

Qwilleran decided this would be the easiest column he had ever written. He turned off the tape recorder and strolled down to the creek.

As he approached it, there were sounds of jubilation. Three persons in front of Cabin Three were laughing and crowing and flinging their arms wide: Hannah and a young couple in jeans. The boy from Cabin Two looked on wistfully until his mother called him away.

"What goes on here?" Qwilleran called out.

All three talked at once. "Good news! She's gone! . . . The airport limo picked her up! . . . Free at last! We're gonna celebrate!"

Hannah made the introductions. They were Wendy and Doyle Underhill from Cabin Three. They recognized the author of the "Qwill Pen." They had enjoyed the column on skeeters. Was it true that only female mosquitoes bite?

Wendy said, "That's why Doyle gets bitten so much. It's his sex appeal!"

Both young people were vibrantly attractive. She had a tumble of dark hair and merry eyes; he looked wholesomely healthy like a camp counselor.

Doyle said, "I like the name of your newspaper."

Wendy said, " I love your slogan!"

Boxed in a corner of the masthead were three words: "There's Always Something!"

Qwilleran explained his mission:

"Today I'm taking the public pulse on the squirrel situation."

"Ask him anything," said Wendy, giving her husband a playful shove. "He's an expert on wildlife."

"Not an expert, but I read a lot."

"Then how do you explain the squirrel's penchant for gnawing power lines and roof shingles?"

"They have to gnaw—or die. Their front teeth, the incisors, actually grow as much as six inches in a year if they don't grind them down. They have an instinct for substances that make efficient grindstones."

Wendy said, "I like having them around,

but I don't encourage them with peanuts, or anything like that."

Hannah said, "They don't bother me. I think they don't like Gilbert and Sullivan. But I saw something amazing one day. A squirrel was floating across the creek on a piece of tree bark or something. I couldn't believe it! I think he was using his tail for a sail. I wish I'd had a camera."

"May I quote this?" Qwilleran asked.

"But don't use my name. Some people think I have a crackpot hobby; they'll think I'm over the edge. . . . Why don't we sit on my porch and have some lemonade?"

They moved to Cabin One.

Wendy said, "I'd love to photograph squirrels racing and chasing each other and running up trees and flying through the branches. Then I'd edit the film to synchronize with Schubert's *Impromptu in F Minor*—perfect squirrel music! Then I'd do a rabbit film to his *Klavierstücke in C*—perfect hippity-hop music."

"One question," Qwilleran asked. "If squirrels are so agile, why are there so many dead ones on the highway?"

"I just happen to know the answer," said

Doyle. "They're quite comfortable with parked cars, but they panic when they meet a moving car, and they try to get up a tree. But it has to be a familiar tree! They're territorial creatures. They'll fight with another squirrel to protect their own territory. . . . so we have this squirrel running to avoid an approaching vehicle, but there's a Murphy's Law for Squirrels: *One's personal tree is always on the other side of the road!* He dashes in front of the car and—another dead squirrel on the highway . . . My next lecture will be at . . ."

Qwilleran asked the Underhills how they planned to celebrate their neighbor's absence. They said:

"We'll whoop and holler and play loud music."

"We'll roast hot dogs on our smoky charcoal stove—bacon-wrapped to make more smoke."

"We'll do wild dances on the beach, half naked."

Hannah said, "Count me out of that one—please! But I'll make cole slaw."

Wendy asked, "How about joining the party, Mr. Qwilleran?"

He replied solemnly, "Mr. Qwilleran went home early. I'm Qwill, his doppelganger." A remark that brought trills of laughter. "Yes, I'd like to join your celebration if you'll let me provide the beverages and keep my clothes on."

At six o'clock he arrived at the party with beer, iced tea and fruit drinks in a bucket of crushed ice. A rustic picnic table was set with paper plates. Doyle presided over the smoking charcoal stove, and Wendy played a Tchiakovsky recording at full volume.

When they sat down, Doyle proposed a toast to the terrible-tempered Mrs. T. "May she stay in Milwaukee until her house is finished. One night I dreamed I pushed her off the Old Stone Bridge, and when I woke I was profoundly disappointed."

Hannah questioned the causes of the woman's crankiness, and the group suggested rotten childhood, lack of love life, hormone imbalance, genes and so forth.

Then they considered the asocial family in Cabin Two. They had apparently gone out to dinner. Hannah said she knew them only as Marge and Joe. Wendy thought they had gotten Danny from a rent-a-kid agency. Doyle said she had a runaway imagination. A photographer by trade, he hopped around taking snapshots of the group.

Then Qwilleran said he would rent Cabin Five as soon as the police released it.

"You'll have no squirrel trouble," Doyle said. "They're wary of cats."

Finally they discussed the opera being performed by the Mooseland chorus. The Underhills were attending Friday night, also, and Qwilleran invited the three of them to be his guests at dinner on Sunday after the last matinee.

Doyle said, "I find Mooseville and Moose County on the map but no Mooseland."

"It was the name given to a new confederated high school," Qwilleran explained. "Now it's a label for anything on the fringes of the county, surrounding the urban core."

"Urban core!" Wendy laughed. "You must be kidding."

"That's where everything happens!

Pickax City, population three thousand, is the county seat. Sawdust City is our industrial capital, also known as Mudville. The center of aggie business is Kennebeck."

Aggie. It amused him to talk like a man of the soil.

"Are there any teaching jobs here?" she asked.

"Always. Teachers die, get kidnapped, skip the country."

"Any movies?" Doyle asked.

"There's a film society, but the original Pickax Movie Palace is now a warehouse for household appliances."

Wendy said, "That what's so enchanting about Moose County. A few miles from your 'urban sprawl' you have a dark, scary forest straight out of Grimm's fairy tales."

"That's the Black Forest Conservancy, established by the K Fund for ecological reasons."

The Underhills approved.

"I hear a truck," Harriet said. "I think it's the folks in Cabin Two. We ought to invite them for a beer, just to be neighborly."

The family of three joined the group. Joe worked hard to be friendly, but Marge was shy, and Danny was tongue-tied.

After the party broke up, Wendy revised her opinion. Danny was Marge's kid, but Marge and Joe weren't married.

To cap the evening, Qwilleran distributed copies of Tuesday's paper. "Read all about it!" he shouted. "Miniaturist discovered at Nutcracker Inn! Inside story of an amazing hobby. Don't miss it in today's *Something*!"

Hannah was on the verge of tears. "I wish Jeb were here. He'd be so proud of me."

After the hot dogs and cole slaw and iced tea, Qwilleran had a strong desire for a cup of coffee and piece of pie. It was after nine o'clock, and a velvet rope was stretched across the entrance to the dining room. But there were diners lingering over their dessert, and the host said he could accommodate Mr. Q. "Sit anywhere," he said.

A server passed, carrying a birthday

cake with a single candle burning. It was en route to a table occupied by three members of the Brodie family. He followed it.

"You're just in time, Qwill!" cried Fran. "Pull up a chair! It's Mother's birthday."

Police chief Andrew Brodie was looking self-conscious in the suit, shirt, and tie he always wore to church. His wife, a modest north-country woman, looked uncomfortable in a dress obviously chosen by her sophisticated daughter.

"Happy birthday!" Qwilleran said. "This is an unexpected pleasure." He clasped her extended hand in both of his.

"Oh, it's such an honor to have you at my birthday party!" she said.

"The honor is all mine. I've heard so much about you!"

"I read your column every Tuesday and Friday, Mr. Qwilleran."

"Please call me Qwill. I don't know your first name."

"Martha, but everyone calls me Mattie."

"Do you mind if I call you Martha? It has a lovely sound, and there are so many famous Marthas in history."

"*Mother!* Will you make a wish and blow out the candle before it sets fire to the cake?" Fran gave Qwilleran a look of feigned exasperation.

He chuckled. Anyone as glamorous and successful as Fran deserved to be exasperated once in a while. When Mrs. Brodie made her silent wish, he could guess what it was—that Fran would marry the president of MCCC and settle down, like the other daughters in the family.

"This is the most wonderful birthday I've ever had!" she confided to Qwilleran. "Dr. Prelligate sent me a dozen long-stemmed red roses—first time in my life! He would have been here tonight but he had to go out of town."

"*Mother!* You're supposed to cut the cake."

The cake was lemon coconut, and Andy announced that Mattie could bake a better one.

Fran asked, "What are you doing here?"

"Snooping. Do you know what happened to the cuckoo clock that was here before old Gus died?"

"There was no cuckoo clock when I started the inventory."

Andy asked, "How do you like staying here?"

"We're on the third floor, and the cats don't like being cooped up, but we can't get into our cabin because the detectives have it sealed."

"Looking for clues," Andy muttered.

Qwilleran huffed into his moustache. "They've had forty-eight hours! Koko came up with one in five minutes!"

"I always said that smart cat should be on the force!"

"Are you going to the opera Friday night? It's the one with the famous cop song: *A policeman's lot is not a happy one!*"

"You ain't kiddin'."

Upstairs, in 3FF, Qwilleran broke the good news to the Siamese. "Soon we'll be moving to a cabin with a screened porch—and ducks paddling, trout leaping, squirrels squirreling!"

He was feeling in good spirits himself, and he composed a limerick to amuse readers of Friday's column.

An amazing young fellow name Cyril
Was ingenious, agile and virile.
He ran up and down trees
On his hands and his knees
And eventually married a squirrel.

chapter six

As Qwilleran was going into the dining room for breakfast, Nick Bamba hailed him from the office. "Couple of things for you here, Qwill. One looks like the postcard from Polly you've been waiting for."

To exhibit his nonchalance, he put the postcard in his pocket and borrowed a paper knife to open the envelope. It contained a pair of complimentary tickets, fifth row on the aisle, for the opening of *Pirates of Penzance*.

At the entrance to the dining room the hostess on duty was Cathy, the MCCC student.

"Would you save me a table for four Sunday evening?"

"In the window as usual?"

"Please. And how are reservations coming in for Friday?"

"Very well! Is there something special?"

"It's opening night of the Gilbert and Sullivan opera at the auditorium. I'm reviewing it for the paper and have two complimentary tickets. Do you know anyone who could use the other one?"

"I'm quite sure. Is it a good opera?"

"Very clever. Very tuneful."

"I'll see what I can do."

He gave Cathy the second ticket, wondering what young innocent would be his seatmate and wishing Polly were in town.

And after taking a table, and after some badinage with the waitress, and after deciding on French toast and sausage patties . . . Qwilleran looked at Polly's first postcard.

He expected to see a replica of an eighteenth-century village with an oxcart on a dirt road, surrounded by hens pecking in the ruts. Instead he saw an airport motel with a hundred-foot electric sign and a parking lot filled with cars. The message on the reverse side was in minuscule handwriting:

Dear Qwill—Arrived safely. Luggage lost.
Delivered in middle of night. Locks broken.
Mona went to hospital with rhinitis caused
by strong perfume on plane.

Love, Polly

Qwilleran huffed into his moustache. He
had asked for more personal news, and
Polly always aimed to please.

Around noon Qwilleran set out for his
luncheon-interview with Bruce Abernethy. The doctor lived in the village of
Black Creek. There were two Black
Creeks, one wet and one dry, as the locals
liked to say. The former flowed north to the
lake and had been a major waterway in pioneer days, when the forests were being
lumbered. It was wider and deeper in the
nineteenth century and had the advantage
of being straight—an important consider-
ation when logs were being driven downstream in the spring. The "dry" half of the
metaphor was the village on the east bank
of the creek—although not completely
dry; the Nutcracker Inn had a bar license,

and there was a neighborhood pub behind the gas station. It had a roller-coaster history: a thriving community in the boom years; a bed of ashes after the Big Burning of 1869; a veritable phoenix in the Nineties; a ghost town after the economic collapse. During Prohibition there was a period of prosperity as rum runners brought their contraband from Canada and went up the creek to the railroad.

When Qwilleran first arrived in Moose County from Down Below, the Limburger mansion stood like a grotesque monument to the past, but there was little else. Now Black Creek's downtown had a post office, fire station and branch bank—plus a drugstore selling hardware, a grocery selling books and flowers, a gas station selling hamburgers, and a barbershop selling gifts.

Qwilleran, on his way to the Abernethy house, stopped to buy flowers, which he handed to the doctor's wife when she greeted him at the door. "Come in! Bruce is on the phone. . . . Oh, thank you! How did you know that daisies are my favorite? . . . The date of the MCCC luncheon has been set for July 27. That's a Thursday. Is that agreeable with your busy schedule? Everyone is so pleased you've consented to join us!"

"My pleasure," he murmured. The invitation was more welcome than he revealed.

The MCCC faculty had not crossed paths with the "Qwill Pen" columnist—nor had he pursued them. His fellow journalists considered them cliquish. Actually the college had a limited curriculum, and many members of the faculty commuted from Down Below to teach two or three days a week. Qwilleran had met the college president briefly when the man was escorting Fran Brodie to a reception. Otherwise, his sole contact was Burgess Campbell, who gave a lecture course in American history. A localite, Campbell frequented the men's coffee shops that were a part of the Moose County culture.

So the invitation to the luncheon was welcome. Contacts made there might open up a new source of "Qwill Pen" material.

Nell was saying, "You're going to love Bruce's story. He's told it only twice, I think, outside the family, so it will be more or less an exclusive for your book. When do you expect to have it published?"

"As soon as I have enough tall tales to make a decent showing—not just 'a slender volume,' as the reviewers say." He was trying not to stare above Nell's head; there was a cuckoo clock on the foyer wall.

"Will it be illustrated?" she asked.

"That possibility hasn't been discussed as yet, but it would help flesh out the volume and add to its desirability."

"I've done illustrating for magazines and would like to submit samples."

"By all means, do it!" Qwilleran said with sincerity.

The doctor came hurrying from his study. "Sorry about the delay. Full speed ahead—to the Black Bear Café! It's my treat."

"I'll drive," Qwilleran said. As they pulled away, he added, "Pleasant neighborhood here. Any problem with squirrels?"

"Not since we frustrated them by putting power lines and cables underground. And notice that the trees are away from the house. There's a brook back there and

some fine black walnuts. They like proximity to water . . . so we have the problem
licked. Until next week! Then their engi-
neering minds will figure out a solution.
There's nothing like a squirrel for keeping
you humble!"

Qwilleran said, "Andy Brodie tells me
you're a fourth-generation doctor."

"And proud of it! My great-grandfather
arrived on a sailing vessel from Canada in
the early days of lumbering here. It was
dangerous work. Axes, saw blades, falling
trees and murderous fistfights took their
toll. Every community had a sawmill, a
rooming house and an undertaker who
built pine coffins. And there were a lot of
amputations in those days. The term 'Dr.
Sawbones' was no joke. As families
moved in, there were children's diseases
and the perils of childbirth. Visit an old
cemetery, and you'll be amazed at the
number of women who died in their twenties. My grandfather—second generation—made house calls on horseback and
did surgery by lamplight in homes that
weren't very clean. My father had an office
in his front parlor, and patients came to

him. He not only treated their ailments but tried to educate them about health and hygiene."

The Black Bear Café was in the town of Brrr, so named because of a sign writer's slip-of-the-brush. Since it was the coldest spot in the county, the townfolk relished the humor of the mistake and enjoyed the distinction of a place-name without a vowel. The town was on a bluff overlooking a fine natural harbor, and on the crest was an old hotel dating from the lumbering era. Architecturally it was in the shoebox style— plain, with many small windows. Its notable feature was a sign that ran the length of the roof, announcing ROOMS . . . FOOD . . . BOOZE. The letters were large enough to be seen for miles, and it was a favorite hangout for boaters, who nicknamed it the Hotel Booze.

Gary Pratt was the present owner, a young man with a lumbering gait and shaggy black beard. It was no wonder the café bore the name it did. When he acquired a mounted black bear as official greeter at the entrance, the picture was complete. Added to the restaurant's attractions was its famous "bear burger," considered the best ground-beef sandwich in the county. Certainly it was the largest.

"What's the Abernethy clan connection?" Qwilleran asked when they had taken seats in a booth.

"Leslie of Aberdeenshire, dating back to the thirteenth century. Nell likes me to wear the kilt. Why don't we promote a Scottish Night at the Nutcracker Inn?"

"Andy could play the bagpipe," Qwilleran suggested.

"My daughter could dance the Highland Fling."

Bruce ordered a glass of red wine, and Qwilleran ordered coffee. Both said they would have burgers—but not right away. They had business to discuss.

Qwilleran produced his tape recorder, and the doctor recounted a story that was later transcribed as "The Little Old Man in the Woods."

When I was eleven years old, we were living in a wooded area outside Fishport, and behind our property was the forest primeval—or so I thought. It was a dense grove of trees that had a sense of mystery for an eleven-year-old. I used to go there to get away from my younger siblings and read about flying saucers. A certain giant tree with a spreading root system above ground provided comfortable seating in a kind of mossy hammock.

I would sneak off on a Saturday afternoon with the latest science fiction magazine—and a supply of pears. You see, the early French explorers had planted pear trees up and down the lakeshore. To own "a French pear tree" was a mark of distinction. We had one that was still bearing luscious fruit. Before leaving on my secret Saturday reading binge, I would climb up into the tree and stuff my shirtfront with pears. Then I'd slink away into the forest.

One day I was lounging between the huge roots of my favorite tree and reading in pop-eyed wonder about the mysteries of outer space, when I heard a rustling in the tree above me. I looked up, expecting a squirrel, and saw a pair of legs dangling from the mass of foliage: clunky brown shoes, woolly brown knee socks, brown leather breeches. A moment later, a small man dropped to the ground—or rather floated to earth. He was old, with a flowing gray moustache, and he wore a pointed cap like a woodpecker's, with the brim pulled down over his eyes. Most amazingly, he was only about three feet tall.

I wanted to say something like: Hello . . . Who are you? . . . Where did you come from? But I was absolutely tongue-tied. Then he began to talk in a foreign language, and I had seen enough World War II movies to know it was German.

Now comes the strangest part: *I knew what he was saying!* His words were being interpreted by some kind of mental telepathy. He talked—in a kindly way—and I listened, spellbound. The more I heard, the more inspired and excited I became. He was talking about trees! That the tree is man's best friend . . . It supplies food to eat, shade on a sunny day, wood to burn in winter, boards to build houses and furniture and boats . . . The greatest joy is to plant a tree, care for it, and watch it grow. What he did not say was something I had learned in school: That trees purify the air and contribute to the ecology of the planet!

Then, before I knew it, he was gone! But I had changed! I no longer wanted to be an astronaut; I wanted to grow trees!

I ran home with my two remaining pears and my magazines, which no longer interested me.

My father was in his study. "What is it, son? You look as if you've had an epiphany." He was always using words we didn't know, expecting us to look them up in the dictionary. I'm afraid I never did.

With great excitement I told him the whole story. To his credit as a parent, he didn't say I had fallen asleep and dreamed it—or I had eaten too many pears—or I had read too many weird stories. He said, "Well, son, everything the old fellow said makes sense. If we don't stop destroying trees without replacing them, Planet Earth will be in bad trouble. Why don't you and I do something about it? We'll be business partners. You find a forester who'll give us some advice about tree farming. I'll supply the capital to buy seedlings. And you'll be in charge of planting and maintenance."

My father was a wise man. One thing led to another, and I became a partner in his medical clinic, just as he had been my partner in growing trees. But that's not the end of the story. In med school I studied German as the language of science, and that's where I met my future wife. We went to Germany on our honeymoon—to practice our second language. I particularly wanted to visit the Black Forest.

In a shop specializing in woodcarvings, I suddenly looked up and saw the little old man who had communicated with me in the woods. He had a long flowing moustache and a Tyrolean hat with the brim pulled down over his eyes, and he was carved from a rich mellow wood with some of the tree bark still visible on the hat.

"*Was ist das*?" I asked.

"A wood spirit," the shopkeeper answered in flawless English. "He inhabits trees and brings good luck to those who believe in him. This one was carved by a local artist."

"How did he know what a wood spirit looks like?" Nell asked.

The shopkeeper looked at her pityingly. "Everyone knows."

I wanted to tell him I'd had a close encounter with a wood spirit but held my tongue—to avoid another pitying look. The carving now hangs over my fireplace, reminding me of the day that changed my life. Was I hallucinating? Or had I eaten too many pears? Or what?

"A compelling story!" Qwilleran said. "I'd like to see your carving of a wood spirit."

"Let's skip dessert and go home for coffee and Nell's black walnut pie."

On the way back to Black Creek, Qwilleran inquired about the strong local interest in the black walnut.

"The tree has always flourished in this area and certain midwestern states, but when the Limburger mansion was built, black walnut furniture and woodwork was highly desirable, and the groves were lumbered out. Today there's a renewed demand for boards and veneer, especially in the Asian market. But it takes good heartwood to make good veneer, and black walnut trees are slow to mature. A good straight tree of the proper age can be worth upwards of fifty thousand. I've planted a grove of black walnuts, interspersed with other hardwoods, as a legacy for my grandchildren."

"Fascinating subject," Qwilleran murmured. "What is your source of information?"

"A friend of mine, Bob Chenoweth, wrote a painstakingly researched book on the subject. You might like to borrow it. He's a good writer."

"The name sounds Welsh." Qwilleran prided himself on knowing the origin of surnames. "Does he sing? You know what they say: All Welshmen sing. All Scots are thrifty. All Englishmen have stiff upper lips. And all Irishmen write plays."

"First," said Qwilleran, when they reached the doctor's house, "I want to see the wood spirit."

The carving hung on the chimney breast, high over the fireplace mantel—craggy face, hooded eyes, long flowing moustache. The artist had brought it to life. "Looks a lot like me when I need a trim," he said.

Then came the black walnut pie! He was familiar with other nut pies and found he disliked their cloying sweetness. Nell's pie had an earthy nuttiness with a texture of creamy chewiness. Qwilleran, though never at a loss for words, could only murmur an enraptured "Wow!"

"Good, isn't it?" Bruce said. "She makes it all the time. I crack the nuts."

"Black walnut is an acquired taste," she said. "Our whole family is hooked on it."

"How large a family?"

"Three daughters. The youngest is in Nova Scotia right now, winning prizes for Scottish dancing."

Bruce said, "The middle one is entering med school. The eldest—" He whipped out his wallet and showed a snapshot of a young woman in tan overalls, bright yellow shorts, slouch hat and field boots. She was standing next to a large tree trunk

with bark peeled down like a banana—
lightning damage. With obvious pride
Bruce said, "She has a degree in forestry.
She works as a forest ranger for the state.
With the growing public concern about
forests, she'll go far!" Then, to veil his
parental pride, he quipped, "She's the one
on the left."

Qwilleran thought, Inside the dedicated
pediatrician, a wood spirit is trying to get
out!

A cuckoo clock sounded the hour. There
were compliments, thanks, promises and
reminders, and Qwilleran left with a copy
of *Black Walnut* under his arm. For a moment he wondered if fate had deprived
him of certain blessings: a father, a loving
wife, talented offspring, concern for future
generations, and black walnut pie "all the
time."

chapter seven

"Good news!" were the first words Qwilleran heard Thursday morning. Nick Bamba called to say that the police had released Cabin Five. "The house-cleaning crew is down there now, giving it a thorough once-over."

"Not too thorough, I hope," Qwilleran said. "Koko likes a few lingering odors. He might detect a clue that has been over-looked by the detectives. I'm not contending that cats are smarter than people, but *some cats* are smarter than *some people*—with all due respect to the constabulary. . . . When can we move down there?"

"Give them another hour. Also, there's a postcard here for you."

Hanging up the phone, Qwilleran said to the cats, "Pack your bags!" They seemed to know what was afoot. Koko pranced around on his long elegant legs. Yum Yum cowered.

Polly's card proved to be from Colonial Williamsburg. Pictured was a company of British redcoats marching down Duke of Gloucester Street.

Dear Qwill—The Governor's Palace is gorgeous! Heard a wonderful concert at the church. Mona okay. Met interesting antique dealer from Ohio.

Love, Polly

Qwilleran huffed into his moustache and wondered what made an antique dealer "interesting." Especially . . . one from Ohio.

Just as Qwilleran was approaching his French toast and sausage patties with gusto, the server came to the table with a cordless phone. "Call for you, Mr. Qwilleran. Will you take it at the table?"

"No. I disapprove of using a phone while operating a knife and fork. Get the name and phone number, and I'll call back after my second cup of coffee."

The number Qwilleran was given to call was Roger MacGillivray's home phone. It was Thursday. He worked weekends at the newspaper in order to have Wednesdays and Thursdays off for home-schooling his youngsters. And on those two days Sharon did freelance bookkeeping for the motel in Mooseville. It was a neat arrangement.

"Roger! You called!" Qwilleran said when his friend answered. "What's up?"

"Would you like to attend a rehearsal of the Reenactors Club? They're doing a reenactment of an 1860 event, and they've hired me as a history consultant. It's been a challenge. A performance will be given every Saturday night in July as a tourist attraction."

"Does the show have a name?" Qwilleran asked.

"'Saturday Night Brawl at the Hotel Booze.'"

"Does the sheriff know about it? He may close it down after the first performance."

"It's a clean show—historic, educational."

"What time is the rehearsal?"

"Eight o'clock."

"Why not come and have dinner with me at the Nutcracker, Rog? I want to hear more about this."

Now came the job of moving to Cabin Five. As soon as Qwilleran produced the first item of luggage, Yum Yum disappeared under the bed. A flashlight showed her huddled under the exact center of the king-sized bed. Cats have an innate spatial sense. Yum Yum knew she was safe. Even the magic word ("Treat!") had no effect. She stayed where she was, and Koko polished off her portion. Her eyes glowed like electric lights when she faced the flashlight.

Then Trent, the porter, arrived to take everything down on the elevator. "All set to go, Mr. Qwilleran?"

"All except one cat."

"No problem! That bed's on casters. Just roll it out from the back wall."

The bed rolled forward, and Yum Yum moved with it; she was still in the exact center.

"What's your next clever suggestion, Trent?" Qwilleran asked.

"Tear gas. Stun gun."

"How about a broom? You make a few swipes under the bed, and I'll catch her when she runs out."

It was a good idea that didn't work. She shot out from the foot of the bed like a cannonball into the turret room and up the spiral staircase.

Trent, hot on her trail, yelled "Gotcha!" and made a grab, just before she launched into space with all four legs spread like a flying squirrel. But Qwilleran knew her flight pattern and caught her like a receiver catching a pass on the ten-yard line. She went limp and was dropped into the cat carrier.

"That little devil!" Qwilleran said. "She likes to make us look like fools. . . . Thanks, Trent. I'll call you again when I need an expert cat-catcher."

Qwilleran unloaded the van at the back door of Cabin Five. Koko, who had been there before, walked in with catly insouciance. Qwilleran showed them the location of their commode and water bowl and served a token treat.

A knock on the porch door sent both cats into hiding.

"Welcome to Creektown," said Wendy, carrying a jug of iced tea.

"Where are the wonderful kitties?" asked Hannah, who had a plate of cookies.

They sat on the screened porch, and Qwilleran inquired about Doyle.

"When he isn't biking he takes a canoe up the creek and shoots pictures of wildlife."

"And what do you do, Wendy?"

"I play stereo recordings of classics and work on the family history I'm writing. My great-grandmother left a trunkful of correspondence going back to the Civil War: hardships, love affairs, disasters, war heroes, and one who disgraced the family by being a bounty-jumper—on both sides! Before the telephone, people wrote long letters in fine handwriting, usually very formal and sometimes poetic, as if they expected their words to be saved for publication. They would say, 'Once more, dear, dear cousin, I take pen in hand and wing my thoughts to you across the miles.' It's an eye-opening adventure for me!"

"I wish someone would write a history of the Scotten and Hawley families," Hannah said, looking hopefully at Qwilleran.

Don't volunteer, he told himself, although he would like nothing better. The great body of water off the coast of Moose County, where the fisheries made their livelihood, was a vast source of drama. Someday he would write a book . . .

"Yow!" came a loud comment from indoors, and the visitors took it as a cue to take their jug and plate and go home.

Cabin Five was compact but well planned, mixing a rustic efficient ambiance with space-saving modern built-ins and plenty of storage space. The bunk room, for example, had two built-in bunks on opposite walls, a closet with no door but plenty of hooks and hangers, open shelves in every spare corner, and a bank of drawers operating on nylon rollers. Easy-gliding drawers were also a feature of the tiny kitchen, dinette, and entertainment center. Table and benches for dining were built-in, as was the upholstered seating in the living room. Altogether, it was snug but comfortable and efficient, like the cabin of a boat. The Siamese seemed to prefer it to 3FF.

As Qwilleran was finding appropriate places for his belongings, he became aware of scurrying sounds under one of the bunks, as if a cat were playing with a mouse.

"Koko! What are you doing?" he demanded, as he beamed a flashlight under a bunk.

The cat was fussing with a pair of shoes, apparently the same pair that had attracted him on his previous tour of inspection. Dislodging them with a broom, Qwilleran found them to be the same brown oxfords, fairly new. "Sorry. Not my size," he said as he sat down to think.

He had attributed Koko's earlier fascination with the shoes to . . . foot powder? Or new leather? Obviously the cat had stashed the shoes away for future reference. Did he sense he was going to return? That cat's ability to predict events was unnerving. . . . And now he had a sudden interest in the area behind the cabins. Apparently he knew that the air-port limousine was coming down the hill and would deliver Mrs. Truffle to Cabin Four.

Qwilleran went on unpacking and putting things away: typewriter and writ-ing materials on the dinette table, books on a wall-hung shelf over the sofa, Koko's harness and leash in a kitchen drawer, the brown oxfords in a drawer under the TV. He was meeting Roger at five-thirty, and he had to freshen up and feed the cats.

At the inn Roger's gray van was pulling into the parking lot, and they went to the dining room together.

The hostess who seated them seemed to know Roger, and he said, "Cathy! Will you be able to get to rehearsal tonight?"

"Yes. Mrs. Bamba is letting me leave at seven-thirty."

Qwilleran's curiosity was piqued. "You'll

have to tell me what this reenactment is all about. How is Cathy involved?"

"She's one of our dance hall girls. . . . That's what we're calling them, anyway."

Roger was a young man with a growing family who seldom went out to dinner except to "Grandma's," meaning Mildred Riker. So Qwilleran urged him to order from the high end of the menu, saying, "It'll go on my expense account, Rog."

Gradually the scenario for the "Saturday Night Brawl" evolved. Roger said, "The year is 1860, and the community of North Cove, now the town of Brrr, is a world of lumber camps, log drives, sawmills, and tall-masted sailing ships. It's a Saturday night in spring, and the saloon at the Hotel Booze is filled with lumberjacks, sawyers and sailors. Upstairs they can stay overnight for a quarter, in a room without a bed but with enough floor space for a dozen men.

"In the saloon there is drinking and gambling and flirting with girls who hang around. Arguments lead to fistfights. Drunks are carried out to sober up on the wooden sidewalk."

"And you're staging this in the Black Bear Café?" Qwilleran asked.

"Yep! The audience sits in the booths on three sides of the restaurant. The action takes place at the long bar and at the tables in the center of the room. The cast is divided into teams of two or three at the bar . . . three or four at the tables. Each team does its thing: card playing, crapshooting, womanizing, Indian wrestling—whatever . . . Got it, Qwill?"

"Got it!"

"Thornton Haggis worked out the staging and plays the saloonkeeper. During the performance he subtly directs the action, so that each team has its moment, and it isn't total chaos."

"Who are the members of the club?"

"Mostly young men, plus a few sisters and girlfriends. My job is to acquaint them with life as it was lived, when this whole area was nothing but dense forest. French traders were the first explorers. Then logging companies came from Maine and Canada. They set up lumber camps in the backwoods, felled trees, floated them down the creeks to sawmills that were set up wherever there was water power."

"What kind of trees did they cut?" Qwilleran asked, thinking of black walnut.

"Pine was king in those days! Pine boards were shipped Down Below because of the building boom in cities. Also, the straight, slender trees, more than a hundred feet tall, made great masts for schooners. Do you realize that *winter* is when trees were harvested? Lumberjacks lived in primitive camps in the backwoods, felled the trees, dragged them out of the woods to ice-covered 'skid roads,' where they were loaded on sledges drawn by ox-teams, and stockpiled on the bank of a frozen creek. When the spring thaw came, they were floated downstream to the sawmills."

Steaks and baked potatoes were served, and the men concentrated on eating, with scraps of information surfacing between bites: "Sawdust cities consisted of a sawmill, boarding house, saloon and undertaker. . . . 'River-drivers' were the daredevils who rode the logs down rushing streams. . . . Danger was everywhere."

Dinner was interrupted when Nick Bamba rushed into the dining room and whispered in Qwilleran's ear.

Jumping to his feet, Qwilleran blurted, "Something's happened to Yum Yum!" He hurried from the room.

"I'll go with you!" Nick said.

"How did you find out?"

"Someone phoned. The Underhills, I think."

The two men were running down the back road—the shortcut.

"What did they say?"

"A cat howling bloody murder."

Qwilleran had the door key in his hand. There was not a second to lose. The howls could be heard.

Then—when they approached the cabin, there was sudden silence.

"What . . . happened?" Nick gasped.

"Don't know."

Qwilleran jabbed the key into the lock and burst into the silent cabin. For a few seconds he looked about wildly.

Nick, at his heels, shouted, "Where are they?"

Yum Yum was sitting comfortably atop

the television. Koko was in the side window, sitting tall on the sill, gazing through the screen toward Cabin Four.

At the same time a raucous voice drifted across from the neighbor:

"I don't care *who* you are! I want to speak to the manager! . . . Hello! Are you the manager? Don't ask me what's wrong! You know very well what's wrong! You moved a screaming hyena into the cabin next to me! I won't stand for it! Get me out of here *fast*! Or I'll call the sheriff! . . . No more apologies. Just find me an accommodation at a decent hotel. And a taxi to move my things! And don't think I'm paying for the taxi! . . ."

Nick said, "I'd better get back to the office and help Lori. I'll explain to your dinner guest."

It was not long before the Nutcracker van drove to the back door of Cabin Four, and a porter loaded luggage and numerous cartons of Mrs. Truffle's belongings.

That was Qwilleran's cue to call the office. Lori answered.

"Where did you send her?" he asked.

"We were able to get her a suite at the Mackintosh Inn."

"That's good. Barry Morghan will know how to handle her. He'll send flowers to her room. He'll even take them up himself."

"She'll throw them at him! She's allergic to flowers."

"I'm sorry Koko created a problem, Lori."

"Not at all! He came up with a solution! No one else could get rid of her."

Qwilleran hung up the phone and went looking for Koko. The cat was in the middle of the living room, hunched over a man's brown shoe—for the left foot. Both shoes had been stowed for safekeeping in the entertainment center, but one drawer had been opened—with a touch of a paw, thanks to the nylon rollers. Yet, only the left shoe had been removed.

Qwilleran tapped his moustache. There was a reason why Koko was interested in it. He had a reason for everything he did— often obscure and sometimes questionable. But the gears were always operative in that small cranium.

Removing the other shoe from the drawer, Qwilleran sat down to study the situation. Both shoelaces had been well chewed at one time or another; that had been Yum Yum's contribution. The right and left shoes seemed to be perfectly mated, although . . . when hefted, one in each hand, the left seemed just . . . slightly . . . heavier. Could that be a fact? Could Koko have detected it? Or was it happenstance?

As Qwilleran stared at the cat in speculation, a long-forgotten memory came into focus. He was fresh out of J school on his first day—at his first job—facing his first assignment. He was to go to the Superior Shoe Company, get a good feature story and hand in his copy by the three o'clock deadline. There was no limit on length. "Write what it takes," the editor said.

The longer the piece, the cub reporter felt, the more editorial attention it would command, provided he was not guilty of padding.

The address was in a commercial district—a building occupied by tailors, wholesale jewelers, theater costumers, custom shirtmakers and the Superior Shoe Company. For the first time he took a taxi on an expense account. For the first time he flashed his brand new press card, and the conversation went like this:

"I'm Jim Qwilleran, here to get a feature story. Did the editor notify you?"

"Yep. Have a chair." He was a leathery man of middle age who obviously worked with his hands. He was surrounded by an assortment of small machines.

"May I have your name, sir?"

"Just call me Bill. Don't need any publicity. Just glad to see a good story in the paper. . . . I've got a nephew workin' for *The New York Times.*"

"Interesting shop. How long have you been making shoes?"

The man shrugged. "Twenty years, give or take."

"Do you have a specialty?"

"Yep." He brought a shoe from underneath the counter and casually peeled away the heel lining and other inner mysteries, revealing a cavity in the heel.

"What's the purpose of this kind of construction?" The trick was to ask questions in a matter-of-fact way as if already knowing the answer.

"It's handy for hiding diamonds, gold coins, spare change," he said with a grin.

There had been more to the interview, and Qwilleran rushed back to the office in excitement. Although he sweated blood over the story, he handed it in with a cool swagger, and the editor received it with a cool nod. It was never printed, of course, being an initiation ritual for cub reporters. He never mentioned it to anyone, nor did any other victim, but he often wondered how many interviews Bill had given—and whether he really had a nephew at *The New York Times.*

Now he went to work on Hackett's left shoe, peeling back the sole lining, removing the heel pad and a metal plate, revealing a heel cavity filled with gold nuggets!

Koko had sensed something abnormal about the shoe. Now, having made his point, the cat was in the kitchen lapping up a drink of water.

Qwilleran reassembled the shoe and hid the pair in his luggage, the only cat-proof enclosure in the cabin—except for the refrigerator. The brown oxfords would have to be turned over to the police as evidence. Should he tell them about the secret heel? Or let them find it themselves?

There were several questions to be asked, and he discussed his puzzlement in his personal journal:

Thursday, June 10—I don't know the market value of gold, but the mysterious Mister Hackett had a heelful—and who knows what larger rocks were stashed in the trunk of his forty-thousand-dollar car? . . . Was he a gold prospector posing as a manufacturer's rep—or a roofing salesman whose hobby was gold-digging? . . . Did someone know about his activity? Or was it an incidental encounter? Did he have a partner—or a competitor—who would consider the booty worth killing for? . . . Where did the clobbering take place? Near the creek, no doubt.

Does that mean Hackett was operating in the Black Forest Conservancy? Is that illegal? Is that why he used an alias and falsified his entry on the inn's guest register? . . . Tune in tomorrow.

chapter eight

It was their first night in the cabin by the creek. Qwilleran placed the cats' blue cushion on one bunk. They settled down contentedly, while he retired to the other bunk. Sometime during the night, the arrangement changed; in the morning Qwilleran was sharing his pillow with Yum Yum, and Koko was snuggled into the crook of his knee. So began . . . A Day in the Life of the Richest Man in the Northeast Central United States.

First, he fed the cats and policed their commode.

Next, he phoned the florist in Pickax and ordered an opening-night bouquet to be delivered to Hannah Hawley's cabin. "Something dramatic—with a few leaves—but none of that wispy stuff that florists love," he specified. In accord with

theatre custom, the card was to read
"Break a leg tonight!" He wished no signature. "Let her figure it out!"

Then he walked up the hill for breakfast
at the inn, taking his Friday column to be
faxed.

Nick Bamba said, "I'll put it on the machine right away, Qwill."

"Not so fast! The deadline is noon. If it
arrives early, some itchy-fingered editor
with a blue pencil will get the urge to
change a few words. It's better for the
copy to arrive when they're beginning to
worry about the thousand-word hole on
page two. . . . How's Lori, Nick?"

"Jumping for joy, now that Mrs. Truffle
has moved out."

It flashed through Qwilleran's mind that
Mrs. Truffle had cast the dark shadow over
the inn—not the ill-fated Elsa Limburger.
He asked, "Who are the quiet people in
Cabin Two?"

"The Thompsons. She's recuperating
from an illness. He goes out deep-sea
fishing on the charter boats every day.
They get big lake trout and have it
cleaned, frozen and shipped to one's

home address. At least, he says that's the way it works. . . . Here's another postcard, Qwill."

It was a view of the Governor's Palace at Colonial Williamsburg. Qwilleran dropped it in his pocket with a show of apathy. "What's today's breakfast special, Nick?"

"Frittata with Italian sauce. Very good!"

"As an old friend, would you tell me it was good if it wasn't?" Qwilleran asked to tease him.

"If you don't like it, send it back to the kitchen, and you can have corn flakes on the house!"

In the dining room Qwilleran cast a quick glance at Polly's postcard:

Dear Qwill—The antique dealer took us to lunch today. Charming man. Called home. Cats not eating well. Could you drop in and cheer them up?

Love, Polly

Qwilleran huffed into his moustache. Polly's male cat had only recently learned to tolerate him, and Black Creek was halfway across the county from Indian Village, where Brutus and Catta lived, but . . .

The server came to take his order, and he asked about the breakfast special.

She shuffled her feet and looked dubious. "Well . . . my last customer thought the sausage was too spicy, and the one before that said the frittata was dry, but that was only their opinion."

Qwilleran had ham and eggs and left her the usual twenty percent plus something extra for honesty.

Back in Cabin Five, he phoned the official historian for Moose County. Homer Tibbitt, a nonagenarian, lived with his wife, a young eighty-eight, in a retirement village, the Ittibittiwassee Estates.

Rhoda answered the phone and said, "Speak of the devil! . . . We were just talking about you at breakfast. Homer's having his after-breakfast nap right now—"

"Who's that? Who's that?" came a high-pitched voice in the background.

"The media," she said as she handed Homer the cordless phone.

Affably the two men exchanged derogatory remarks.

"You old rascal! How come you take a nap in the middle of the morning?"

"You sneaky pup! Calling my wife when you think I'm asleep!"

"How do you like this weather?"

"What do I know about weather? She won't let me go out."

"I hear your knee replacement was a big success, Homer."

"So good I'm thinking of having my funny bone replaced, if you're the donor."

Only after the required banter did Qwilleran pose the question: Has Moose County ever had a gold rush?

"Well . . ." Homer mused as he retrieved pertinent facts, "there was a Poor Man's Gold Rush in the nineteenth century before they discovered the real gold: coal and lumber; that's where the fortunes were made.

"In my own lifetime there's been periodic hysteria over a gold strike, but it never amounted to anything. If you ask me, there's more cold cash buried in coffee cans in people's backyards than was ever—"

Rhoda snatched the phone. "Ask Mr. MacMurchie. He used to sell sluice boxes and panning equipment."

Homer snatched it back again. "Ask Thornton Haggis. He used to take his boys panning."

Without delay Qwilleran phoned the retired stonecutter and made an appointment for lunch. Thornton was one of the most savvy natives he had met since coming to the north country. Thorn, as he was called, had attended a university Down Below, majoring in art history before returning to manage the family's monument works. After retirement he plunged into volunteer work—helping at the art center, assisting the sheriff's department in spotting brush fires, and now playing the role of saloonkeeper in the forthcoming reenactment. It came as no surprise to Qwilleran that Thorn had been a gold prospector.

They agreed to meet at the Nasty Pasty

in Mooseville; only a restaurant serving the best pasties in the county could risk such a name. Meanwhile, Qwilleran and the Siamese sat on the screened porch and enjoyed the sylvan quiet.

Koko chattered at an occasional squirrel who had come too close to his turf and pointed his ears toward the creek when he heard quacking. Qwilleran quickly harnessed him and took him for a shoulder-ride down to the water's edge. Two ducks were gliding serenely followed by nine ducklings (he counted them) in perfect formation, the entire company turning left or right like a drill team.

A man's voice said, "Only the females quack; the males go cluck-cluck." It was Doyle Underhill from Cabin Three. "Is this the cat that got rid of Mrs. Truffle? We should give him a medal."

The photographer was heading for the boat shed with his camera. "Do you like canoeing, Qwill? You're welcome to come with me any time."

"Unfortunately, Doyle, I had a traumatic experience while paddling along the shore of the big lake. A sudden offshore breeze spun the prow around to the north, and I was on my way to Canada a hundred miles away. There was nothing I knew to do until a sepulchral voice from nowhere told me to back-paddle. I made it safely back to shore but lost my taste for canoeing."

"Sounds supernatural."

"No, it was only my neighbor on the beach, a retired police chief with a bullhorn. . . . How's the shooting up the creek?"

"Great! The other day I photographed a huge owl, taking off over my head like a bomber."

"What do you do with your photos?"

"Sell a few to magazines and photo services."

"Do you know about the photography show opening Sunday at the Pickax art center? They're having a reception for the artist, John Bushland."

"I see his byline all the time! He's super! I didn't know he lived around here."

"You and Wendy should go and meet him, between two and five o'clock. He likes to be called Bushy because he's losing his hair."

"We'll go. Thanks for the tip. Too bad you don't like canoeing, Qwill. When I'm paddling up this creek I really feel one with nature."

A few minutes later he was paddling quietly upstream without disturbing the ducks.

When Qwilleran arrived at the Nasty Pasty in Mooseville, Thornton Haggis was waiting in a corner booth, his generous shock of snow-white hair making him instantly visible.

"I see your wife hasn't let you go to the barber recently." Qwilleran said, pursuing their usual joke.

"I let her win the battle this time. I'm playing the saloonkeeper in the reenactment, and they think white hair will make the character look like a wholesome father figure."

"How did you get involved?"

"Funny thing. When my boys were teens, they hated history. Now they're two grown men with families and an active sand-and-gravel business, and they were the first to join the re-enactors. They talked me into it."

The two men ordered the café's famous pasty. Thornton said, "I like it because they make the crust with vegetable oil in the new way instead of lard in the old way, and they dice the meat up the old way instead of grinding it in the new way. They use local potatoes and season the filling with sage and onion and a little butter."

"Is cooking one of your many skills, Thorn?"

"No, but I like to read cookbooks."

"Homer tells me you used to go gold prospecting, Thorn."

"That's when my boys were about ten and twelve years old. After that, they got interested in soccer and girls, but for one summer, panning for gold was good, clean, family fun. We found a few crumbs, which we had imbedded in plastic for key rings. I still use mine."

"Where did you go digging—or panning?"

"In what is now the Black Forest Conservancy—and off limits to prospectors. But in those days, you could cut down trees, camp out, shoot deer in season and rabbits all year round. It was called the Black Forest because of the black bears that made their habitat there, but the only one I ever saw is the stuffed specimen at the Black Bear Café. Nowadays, if you were dumb enough to shoot a bear, they'd shoot *you* and stuff you."

The pasties were served, and Qwilleran asked him more questions. "How did you know where to dig for gold?"

"Everyone knew. There was an old belief that three veins of gold ran under the Black Creek, and every generation got excited about it. Then, when no one struck it rich, it would die down until another old codger starting telling stories."

Forks were not served, and the pasties required two hands and one's full attention.

Then Qwilleran said, "Should I know about the brawl at the Hotel Booze?"

"It isn't all rough stuff," Thornton said. "There's laughing, kidding around, singing, jigging, and a lot of boasting. Roger

MacGillivray has done a pile of research and is coaching them on the slang of the period."

"Is there a script?"

"It's all ad lib, but each team has been doing its act over and over again."

"Do guns figure in the show?"

"It wasn't a gun culture. Fisticuffs! In the lumber camps, fighting and drinking were forbidden. The bosses preserved law and order with their fists. However, in the sawdust towns the saloonkeeper would be likely to have a gun for business reasons."

"Do you know some of the lingo?" Qwilleran asked.

Thornton did. That man knew everything. "We've given our members a glossary of slang terms that were common in those days. I've brought you a copy."

Qwilleran glanced at it. If a man was "sluiced," he was killed. If he had "smallpox," he'd been in a fight and had been stomped by caulks—the steel pins loggers wore on their boots to keep from slipping off logs. If a lumberjack was "gonna get m'teeth fixed," he was going to visit a prostitute. There were other expressions, too, all equally colorful.

Thornton said, "When you see the show, bear in mind that lumberjacks in 1860 were young men in their teens and early twenties. One camp had a cook who was only twelve years old. . . . And they lived dangerously. They were killed by falling trees, drowned while riding logs down a rushing stream, and maimed by runaway saw blades in the mills. Undertakers couldn't make the pine boxes fast enough!"

"Is that why they drank themselves silly on Saturday night?" Qwilleran asked.

"And learned to take death lightly. My great-grandfather cut names and epitaphs on gravestones at two bits a word. If the victim had no money in his pocket, his buddies chipped in to buy him a head-stone with the kind of raffish epitaph he would have liked.

"This will explain the finale of the reen-actment when you see it. Some of the audience will be disturbed."

"What is the finale?"

"Wait and see," Thornton said.

Before leaving the parking lot of the Nasty Pasty, Qwilleran phoned his attorney's office. G. Allen Barter was his representative in all matters pertaining to the Klingenschoen Foundation, sparing him trips to Chicago, board meetings and routine decisions. The two men were in complete accord about the goals and policies of the K Fund.

Qwilleran said, "I suppose you have Saturdays off, unlike us overworked columnists."

"I thought you were on vacation, Qwill. When I read your column today, I assumed the squirrels had written it for you!"

"Don't be too surprised. They're smarter than you think."

"Do you have something in mind for Saturday?" Barter asked.

"Yes. Lunch at the Nutcracker Inn. They have the best Reuben sandwich this side of the Hudson River."

"Good! Do I dare inquire of your ulterior motive?"

"I'd like some information on the Black Forest Conservancy."

"Shall I bring the files?"
"Only those between your ears, Bart."

Before leaving for the opera Friday night, Qwilleran played the video that Hannah had lent him. He was familiar with the plot, characters and songs, but it refreshed his memory. Koko was duly impressed, yowling—in either pleasure or pain—at the rousing opening number: *Oh it is a glorious thing to be a pirate king!* Yum Yum expressed her boredom by sitting with her back to the screen and twitching her ears.

No opening night on Broadway could surpass in excitement the event that took place in the auditorium of the Mooseland high school. Everyone dressed for a very special occasion, a few in long dresses and dinner jackets. The lobby was conversational bedlam, since everyone knew someone in the cast: relative, friend, neighbor, coworker, customer, patient or parishioner.

The parking lot was jammed, and Qwilleran used his press card in order to

park with the dignitaries and handi-
capped. The lobby was teeming with
showgoers too excited to go to their seats.
Qwilleran pushed through the crowd, nodding and saluting.

At a table in the lobby, orders were being taken for pirate socks, knee-high and
tri-colored, with proceeds to underwrite
the choral club expenses. The socks, it
was predicted, would become the tourist
fad of the year.

He also indulged in his favorite vice,
eavesdropping:

"I always love the pirates! They're so
friendly!"

"I love the policemen. They're so good-
hearted and a little timid."

"There's Elizabeth Hart. Where's Derek
Cuttlebrink? They're always together."

"There's Dr. Prelligate with that interior
designer."

"Don't look now, but the man with a
moustache is Mr. Q."

As he walked down the aisle to the fifth
row, he wished Polly were there; she knew
the opera by heart. He wondered who
would be sitting next to him—that is, if

Cathy had been able to give his ticket away. To his surprise it was Cathy herself.

"I've never seen an opera, and I decided it would be part of my education."

"This isn't *Pagliacci* or *Tosca,* you know. It's a musical farce. Do you appreciate farce?"

"I don't know. What is it exactly?"

She was frank and eager to learn, and he admired her for that. "It's a comedy in which ridiculous elements are treated seriously. Prepare to suspend your disbelief, your common sense, and even your sanity."

"It sounds like fun," she said soberly. "What's it about?"

"Do you know Penzance?"

"I don't think so."

He had to talk fast. The orchestra members were looking expectant. Latecomers were rushing to their seats. "It's a town on the coast of England, once a hangout for pirates. A youth named Frederick, who was supposed to be apprenticed to a pilot, was mistakenly apprenticed to pirates, because his baby-sitter was hearing-impaired. Now, at the age of twenty-one, he

is being released from his contract. His
baby-sitter, who had been so embar-
rassed that she went into piratical service
with him, also quits and tags along after
her young master. Her role is sung by Hannah Hawley, who is living in one of the
Nutcracker cabins."

"Mrs. Hawley was written up in your column this week!" Cathy exclaimed. "I'd
love to see her doll house things."

Uncle Louie, as the conductor was af-
fectionately known, came to the podium
as the lights dimmed and bowed to the
audience with a mischievous smile. Then
he turned, rapped twice with his baton,
raised both arms, and plunged the orchestra into the overture. The frenzied opening
bars had the audience smiling as they settled in for three hours of bouncy music, a
few romantic melodies, witty lyrics, and a
madcap plot . . . all except Cathy. She
was not sure what to expect or how to react.

The curtain rose on a rollicking band of
pirates on the beach at Penzance, cele-
brating Frederick's release. All wore red
bandannas on their heads—and striped

knee socks hand-knitted for the occasion. Ruth-poor-Ruth, their maid-of-all-work, was padded and costumed to look dumpy and dowdy.

"Is that Mrs. Hawley?" Cathy whispered.

Her solo explaining her mistake was delivered with full-throated verve and conviction, and applause brought down the house—not only because the house was filled with Hawleys and Scottens.

Another favorite was the stuffy major general with his over-trimmed uniform and wooden-soldier gait. His patter song, delivered with the speed of an automatic weapon, also delighted the audience. His beautiful daughters (twelve members of the women's chorus) fluttered about the beach in long dresses, hats and gloves. One of them, a lyric soprano, fell in love with the ex-pirate, a romantic tenor. So far, so good. Qwilleran glanced at Cathy; she was sitting there solemnly, being educated.

Then the problems arose. The other pirates (twelve members of the men's chorus) wanted to marry the major general's daughters. At the same time, an error in reading the fine print of Frederick's contract had released him too soon. And the major general told a heinous lie as the curtain fell on Act One.

These were all twists of plot that sent a happy audience to the lobby for a glass of punch during intermission.

Qwilleran said, "I'm going to the lobby. Would you like to stretch?" He avoided asking her what she thought of the opera, so far. Instead, he said, "Roger Mac-Gillivray tells me you're going to be a dance hall girl in the reenactment. How did you get involved?"

"My boyfriend is playing one of the river-drivers. They came down from French Canada to ride the logs downstream in spring. He teaches romance languages at the high school, so he'll speak French. They wear red sashes and red knitted caps."

"What do the dance hall girls do?"

"Hang around the saloon, and the customers say 'chip, chip' to us. That's the 1860 equivalent of the wolf whistle."

Before he could comment, the Abernethys appeared, and he introduced her as "Cathy of the Nutcracker staff," adding, "Sorry, Cathy, I don't know your last name."

"Hooper, of the Trawnto Beach Hoopers."

Brightly Nell said, "My name was Cooper, from the Purple Point Coopers. My cousin married a Hooper."

"That was my aunt, and I was flower girl. That was the wedding where the cake exploded!" With difficulty, she suppressed giggles.

Nell was overwhelmed with mirth. "It was supposed to shoot off fireworks, but it backfired! The tablecloth caught fire and my cousin poured champagne punch on it!"

"Everyone was screaming!"

"The bride's mother fainted!"

The two women were rocking with laughter, and the two men looked at each other and shook their heads.

Nell regained her composure enough to explain, "The *Pickax Picayune* headlined it 'Hooper-Cooper Nuptials' and didn't say a word about the explosion. Now, whenever there's a big wedding, we call it a real Hooper-Cooper!"

Qwilleran said, "Why don't I find this event funny?"

The women said in unison, "Because you weren't there!"

The lights blinked, summoning the audience back to their seats. As they moved toward the auditorium, Nell said, "Don't forget the MCCC luncheon, Qwill."

"Are you having fireworks?" he asked. He wanted to inquire about her connection with MCCC, but this was not the appropriate time.

As he and Cathy waited for the lights to dim and for Uncle Louie to return to the podium, she asked, "What happens in the second act?"

"Deceit, vengeance, intrigue, and a happy ending. The pirates battle the cops, who win on a technicality." He handed her the lyrics in booklet form. "Take these home and read them, and you'll appreciate W. S. Gilbert's freewheeling way with rhyme. Who else would rhyme *lot of news* with *hypotenuse*?"

"Thank you. Shall I return it?"

"No. It's part of your education."

When the last triumphant chorus ended, the hall exploded in applause, cheers and whistles.

Cathy was glad that the pirates turned out to be decent after all.

"That's Gilbert and Sullivan," Qwilleran said.

"I loved their socks!"

She thought the policemen in their brass buttons and bobby hats were adorable. "But I felt so sorry for Ruth-poor-Ruth!"

"Don't waste your tears. At the end she went off with the police chief and was winking at the audience."

Hannah Hawley was the hit of the show—and not just because the auditorium was packed with Hawleys and Scottens.

Arriving at the cabin, Qwilleran could hear the Howling Chorus even as he put the key in the door. He realized it was not exactly delight at seeing him; it was a reminder that their elevenses were overdue. Automatically, he scanned the premises for catly mischief, just as Nick Bamba scanned a vacated guest room for missing lightbulbs and dripping hot water faucets. There were no shredded newspapers or disarranged pens and pencils, but two items had been pushed off the shelf over the sofa: Hannah's video of *Pirates* and Bruce's copy of *Black Walnut.* The latter reminded him there were some black walnut cookies in the refrigerator, and he brewed a cup of coffee.

chapter nine

On Saturday, Qwilleran was "up be-times," as they used to say three centuries ago. What, he wondered, had happened to that word? It was still in the dictionary. If Polly were there, they would have a lively discussion about it. He missed her most on weekends. Later, he would drive over to her place to cheer up the cats, who missed her too.

Meanwhile he had coffee and a thawed breakfast roll on the porch. The cats were nearby, washing up after their own breakfast when, suddenly, they went on ear-alert. Someone was coming along the creek footpath.

It was the small boy from Cabin Two. He approached the screen saying, "Kitty! Kitty! You found your mittens!"

The cats remained stiffly aloof from this

alien creature who was larger than a squirrel and smaller than a human.

Qwilleran started to say, "Does your mother—?"

"Danny! Danny!" screamed a shrill voice, and a frail-looking woman came hurrying along the path. "I told you not to bother people!"

"I wanna see the kitties!"

She snatched his wrist and dragged him home while he looked back in disappointment.

In preparation for Barter's luncheon visit, he had some exploring to do and was pleased that he had brought his trail bike. The dense woods called the Black Forest Conservancy adjoined the Nutcracker Inn to the south and stretched for miles and miles.

He put on the biking gear that always scared the cats—tight-fitting green-and-purple suit, spherical yellow helmet, large black sun goggles—and wheeled his bike to Cabin One, where he rapped on Hannah's back door.

She greeted him with a small cry of alarm and then laughed.

"Oh, it's you, Qwill! I thought it was someone from outer space. Come in!"

"Not today, thanks. I have miles to bike before noon. Just stopped to say that your ovation last night was well deserved."

"I had a lot of friends in the audience."

"Friends or no friends, you created a believable character, and you have a splendid voice!"

"Thank you," she said graciously, with the aplomb of one who believes in herself.

"We'll talk about it tomorrow night at dinner. I suggest we all meet here and walk up the hill."

Qwilleran pedaled east on Gully Road with farmland on his left and the Black Forest on his right, and he thought about Fanny Klingenschoen. While pursuing a lucrative career on the fast track—elsewhere—she had bought up half of Moose County. She acquired woodland and abandoned mining villages as well as property in downtown Pickax. Ecologically, she was doing something right, but she was doing it for her own reason: revenge against the "respectable" families who had scorned her freewheeling ancestors. Now the wilderness holdings had been placed in conservancy by the Klingenschoen Foundation—to prevent development and do some small part in saving the planet.

In the wrong hands, Qwilleran was aware, millions of trees would have been cleared to make way for high-density condominiums, a golf course, and even an auto raceway. The pure air and water of the north country would have been exchanged for population growth and pollution. He had been reading about trees and oxygen and rain.

The K Fund had established three conservancies, each with its own agenda. The largest, called the Black Forest, was dedicated to the preservation of wildlife, and Qwilleran wanted to gain some idea of its character before discussing it with the attorney.

After a mile or so on Gully Road there came a break in the dense wall of evergreens, hardwoods and other growth. A sign—obviously new but made to look

old—announced BLACK FOREST CONSER-
VANCY—WILDLIFE REFUGE.

There was an entryway of sorts, wide enough for a motor vehicle but hardly more than a beaten path into the woods: weeds, ruts, stones, tree roots, and forest debris. It had no name, only a county number on a leaning pole—with a warning: DEAD END. Qwilleran was curious enough, and his trail bike was sturdy enough, to give it a try.

Actually it appeared to dead-end fifty yards ahead at a lofty outcropping of rock, the kind of souvenir deposited by prehistoric glaciers.

Standing on the pedals and gripping the handlebars with determination he headed for the rock, only to find that County 1124 went around it, turning left, then turning right around the east end of the rock, then turning right again into . . .

"What the devil!" Qwilleran yelped as he came face-to-face, or rather face-to-tail, with a large truck! It had a Wisconsin tag. It looked like an interstate moving van.

He walked his bike around it. The name painted on the side of the van was DIAMOND

MOVING AND STORAGE. The cab window was open, and the driver was talking on a cell phone.

"Having trouble? Are you lost?" Qwilleran asked helpfully.

The man dropped the phone when he saw the yellow bubble-head with goggle eyes and enough facial hair for an old English sheepdog. "Uhh . . . Takin' a break. Been drivin' all night."

"How far have you come?"

"Milwaukee . . . Where's a place to eat?"

"At the gas station in Black Creek. But you can't turn around, and you'll never back out with this rig."

"I done it before."

"Well . . . good luck!"

Qwilleran hopped on his bike and punished the pedals some more, meanwhile thinking he had insulted a professional teamster. He remembered working at a metropolitan newspaper and being fascinated by the flatbed trucks that delivered the giant rolls of newsprint. To back up to the pressroom's loading dock, the driver had to double-jackknife backward—from a busy street to a narrow alley to a narrower dock.

He continued to follow 1124 on its eccentric course around more outcroppings of rock, clumps of trees, evil-looking bogs, and one ancient tree with a trunk at least five feet in diameter. At one point a tree had fallen across the road, and he had to lift his bike over it.

He saw no wildlife larger than a squirrel but heard crackling in the underbrush and rustling in branches overhead. And he could hear the sounds of distant civilization: an emergency siren, shots from a rabbit-hunter's gun, a chain saw turning a tree into firewood, a hammer turning cedar boards into a deck.

At intervals, trails led into the depths of the forest, disappearing into a mysterious darkness suitable for fairy tales about wolves and wicked witches.

When 1124 dead-ended at the creek, Qwilleran had had enough, and he returned to the reality of Gully Road. The moving van had gone, and—he remembered later—there was no fallen tree crossing 1124.

Before the attorney arrived, there was time to shower, give the Siamese their noontime entitlement, and open a bottle of red wine, to breathe. Barter always looked lawyerly, even in jeans, polo shirt, baseball cap and sneakers. He walked into the cabin with authority and appraised the ingenious space-savers and built-ins. "Snug!" was his verdict.

Pompously Qwilleran said, "Think not of it as a small dwelling; think of it as a large boat."

"Where are the cats?"

"Out on deck. If you'll join them and pour yourself a glass of wine, I'll phone the inn to start our sandwiches."

Koko ignored the visitor, but Yum Yum could smell a shoelace at fifty paces and approached stealthily.

"Cheers!" the attorney said, lifting his glass, while his host raised his glass of Squunk water with a dash of cranberry juice.

Barter said, "My wife wants to know if

you're having a limerick contest this summer. She won a prize last year."

"I remember. It was about the town of Brrr. Tell her that public clamor is forcing us to repeat it. Did she ever write a limerick about you, Bart?"

"Yes, and I won't recite it. . . . Now what do you want to know about conservancies, Qwill?"

"I know that wilderness tracts can be legally protected against development. And I know the K Fund has put three tracts in conservancy. The Piney Woods will be open to hunters in deer season; Great Oaks offers campsites for tents but not recreational vehicles—"

"And all campsites are reserved through Labor Day," the attorney interrupted. "It has beach access and thirty miles of beach hiking in each direction. The agate-hunters are enthusiastic."

"But what about the Black Forest, Bart? I biked through it, and nothing's happening."

"That's the largest and most ambitious, Qwill. The idea is to admit hikers and photographers but prohibit hunting, camping,

off-road vehicles and exploitation of natural resources."

"Meaning what?"

"No timbering. No removal of minerals or
plant life. But first they have to take inventory of what we have in the Black Forest.
They're sending in botanists, geologists,
ornithologists—scientists from every dis-
cipline. It's thought that Moose County is
a treasure trove of natural science. It's already known that the Black Forest has
bears, wolves, foxes, bobcats, beaver,
raccoons, skunks, and otters, as well as
deer—"

"And squirrels," Qwilleran added. "How
are you going to keep the tourists from
digging up rare plants, feeding the deer,
setting fire to the woods?"

"All of that's in-work. They hire forest
rangers to monitor the situation and con-
duct educational programs."

A horn tooted at the back door, and a
porter delivered the sandwiches and fries
under hot-covers and coffee in Thermos
jugs. Then the conversation turned to
shoptalk.

Barter asked, "What are your plans for

that hundred-year-old furniture that's in temporary storage?"

"No plans. Only hopes," Qwilleran replied. "It belongs in a museum. Moose County doesn't have one."

"There's the Goodwinter farmhouse."

"Too primitive. What's in storage has class, provenance, quality and beauty. One of the big houses on Pleasant Street would make a suitable museum."

"It would require rezoning. The neighbors would fight it."

Qwilleran said, "The K Fund could build an art center. They should be able to build a museum. Think about it."

Barter stood up to leave. "Great sandwiches. Peaceful scene. I hate to leave."

"I hear you've taken in a new partner. Hasselrich, Bennett, Barter and Adams."

"Mavis Adams from Rochester, Minnesota. Good mind. Nice woman. Likes cats. In fact, she has an idea for a new kind of animal rescue program."

"Bart, your shoelaces are untied," Qwilleran said.

In preparation for his mercy expedition to Indian Village Qwilleran packed a few treats—nothing fancy; Polly's cats were accustomed to a plain diet. His own Siamese watched with concern as *their food* was being put in a plastic tote bag, along with *their necktie.*

"I'm going to see your cousins in Indian Village," he explained. "Do you have a message for them?" They had none. They were simply waiting for him to leave, so they could have their afternoon nap.

Arriving at Polly's condo, Qwilleran let himself in with his own key, and the Siamese came forward promptly, their body language more inquisitive than enthusiastic. He passed muster, but it was obvious they would have preferred Polly. She talked cat-talk. Qwilleran talked about the weather, their health, the cat-sitter. "This treat comes to you with the good wishes of your cousins, vacationing at Black Creek."

They approached the plate cautiously, looked up at him questioningly, then gobbled it up.

Next came the necktie game. "Have you guys been getting any exercise?" He whipped out the frayed necktie, twirled it, dragged it tantalizingly across the floor. "Very interesting," they seemed to say as they watched from nearby chairs.

Finally, Qwilleran read to them from the *Wilson Quarterly*—all about the political situation in Indonesia—and they fell asleep. He tiptoed from the house. He had done it for Polly. What was she doing, he wondered? Probably dressing for dinner with the Ohio antique dealer.

From his car he phoned the Pickax police chief at home.

Brodie's wife answered. "He's in the shower. We're going to Tipsy's. He likes the steak. I like the fish. If we don't go to Tipsy's, we go to Linguini's. . . . Oh, here he is!"

Andy came on the line with an impatient growl, as if he were still dripping.

"This is Qwill, Andy. Would it be worth your while to drive to Black Creek for (a) some good Scotch and (b) a clue to a mystery murder?"

"M'wife and me, we always go out to dinner Saturday night, then watch a video."

"What are you watching tonight?"

"It's her turn to choose. She wants *On Golden Pond.* Third time! I'll be ready for a wee nip! How about eleven o'clock?"

"You know where I am. Cabin Five."

On the way home Qwilleran stopped at the Nutcracker for a piece of black walnut pie and, he hoped, another post-card from Polly.

Lori handed it to him. "I couldn't help looking at the beautiful picture, Qwill—all those schooners in full sail! I'd love to see them! She must be having a wonderful time."

It came from Mystic Seaport, Connecti-cut, and the message read:

Dear Qwill—Sea air! Tall ships! Atmo-sphere of a colonial seaport! Walter intro-duced us to navy grog. Delicious! I feel like dancing!

Love, Polly

Qwilleran huffed into his moustache. She sounded a little tipsy. Was this Walter person leading her astray? Her usual drink was a small glass of sherry, and he had never heard her say that she felt like dancing. Abruptly he asked Lori, "Where's Nick?"

"Supposed to be changing filters in the basement, but he may be fixing a tile on the roof. You know how he is—all over the place." She said it with approval.

Qwilleran tracked him down. "What do you know about navy grog, Nick?"

"It's a drink. Pretty potent, they say."

"Do you know the ingredients?"

"Our barman would, but he isn't on duty yet. We could look it up in his drink manual. . . . Come on."

In the vacant bar Nick found the manual, almost two inches thick, and read, "Jamaica rum, white rum, lime juice, orange juice, pineapple juice, guava nectar, crushed mint leaves, and a teaspoon of Falernum."

"What's Falernum?" Qwilleran asked.

"Never heard of it. Sounds like the West Indies."

"It doesn't sound good," Qwilleran muttered, as he visualized Polly dancing with sailors after a sip or two. "Thanks, Nick!"

Driving downhill to the creek, Qwilleran could hear Hannah doing her vocal exercises, tuning up for the second performance. Behind Cabin Three he could hear one of Wendy's Schubert recordings. Unlocking his own door, he could hear the welcome howls of Koko and Yum Yum. As soon as he walked into the cabin, however, there was sudden silence. They knew where he had been and what he had been doing: fraternizing with the competition!

"Too bad about you!" he said. And he made a cup of coffee.

Later, sitting on the porch in the twilight, Qwilleran reviewed his conversation with the attorney and his excursion into the Black Forest. It had been strenuous, and he was beginning to feel a muscular reaction here and there. There was something magical about a dense forest. He could see how Hans Christian Andersen and the Brothers Grimm had been inspired to write the tales they did! As for himself, now that he was away from the spell of the Black Forest he began to question the presence of the moving van on the scrubby 1124. He wished he had made a note of the license number; Brodie could have put a check on it. The van had gone when he returned from his arduous pedaling. Had it backed out, or had it gone deeper into the woods on one of those half-hidden side trails? And if that were the case, what was its mission? And did that explain why the fallen tree across 1124 had been removed? And had it "fallen" or been placed there?

When Chief Brodie stomped into the cabin, he said gruffly, "Why don't you trade in that antiquated van on a good-looking sports utility vehicle?"

"I like my van. It's been a good old work-horse."

"It's a clunker," Andy insisted. "Gippel has a new shipment of SUVs, and will make you a good deal—just one look and he'll have you drivin' around in one of them. And it would look better for the writer of the 'Qwill Pen.' I'll bet Polly would like the colors."

"Are you on Gippel's payroll?" Qwilleran asked. "Go sit on the screened porch, and I'll bring the tray."

"Have you heard from Polly?" Brodie asked after they were seated at the porch table with drinks and cheese board.

"I get regular postcards. There's an antique dealer who seems to have latched on to her. He's interested in the Duncan heirlooms. Susan Exbridge says they're worth a mint!"

"That guy would try to swindle her for sure. She comes across as a nice lady, but she's tough as nails and he won't get anywhere. . . . So what's the clue you mentioned, Qwill?

"First, have they found out who Hackett really was?"

"They've found out that he wasn't a sales rep selling building supplies to lumber companies and contractors. Nobody ever heard of him—or the company he said he worked for. He was here for some other purpose, probably drug-related."

"But maybe not. Let me show you a pair of shoes he left here. The police overlooked them because they were shoved way under a bunk." Qwilleran produced the brown oxfords. "What do you think of these?"

"Good leather. Expensive." Then he watched with disguised surprise as the inner layers of the left shoe were peeled away, revealing the nuggets of gold in the heel.

"Hmff! Not much of a haul." Brodie observed.

Qwilleran said, "I say this is only a gimmick—something to show friends. I say he was after the big stuff, and they were packed in his car when it was stolen—along with a pickax and diving equipment and a wet suit. Diving for gold is a current craze in other parts of the country, I've read. And, I'm sure you know, the locals have always talked about several veins of gold under the Black Creek. No doubt he was on the bank of the creek when someone hit him on the head and threw him in the water!"

"This would make a good movie—better than the one I saw tonight for the third time."

"No doubt he's been driving his car onto 1124, then down one of the side trails to the creek. Someone knew about it—probably a partner, who knew he was about to leave. Perhaps the partner had come up with Hackett from Down Below."

"Glad to know the skunk was not one of us," Andy said, still reluctant to take the story seriously.

"The question is, why did Hackett falsify everything on the inn's guest register? Because he had found out, somehow, that 'exploitation of minerals' in the Black Forest Conservancy is now outlawed. He was trying to make one more haul before the forest rangers started policing the gold fields. . . . Let me refresh your drink, Andy. . . . Try this Roquefort. It's the real thing."

The chief left with the shoes wrapped in newspaper and instructions to tell state detectives they had overlooked them during the forensic search. "Tell them the innkeeper turned them over to you—and you suspected something fishy about the left shoe. Leave me out of it! . . . Then they can piece together their own scenario. Personally, I think mine was pretty good!"

chapter ten

Although Qwilleran missed his nightly telephone chats with Polly, he missed her most on weekends. Only two Sundays ago they had breakfasted on black walnut pancakes, driven to the lakeshore for a long walk on the strand, dined memorably at the Boulder House Inn—all the while enjoying long discussions about nothing much.

He remembered her telling how she memorized sonnets to recite aloud while doing boring tasks around the house. She knew twenty by heart: Shakespeare ("When to the sessions of sweet silent thought") and Wordsworth ("Earth has not anything to show more fair"). She favored sonnets because they were only fourteen lines, and the rhyme scheme made them easy to memorize. Also, she found the rhythm of iambic pentameter comforting. "If Wordsworth were alive today," she said, "I'd invite him to lunch."

And he remembered her surprise to learn that only four American presidents have found the moustache appropriate: Theodore Roosevelt, Grover Cleveland, Chester K. Arthur, and William Howard Taft. (Arthur had sideburns that all but overshadowed his moustache.) Four presidents had full beards, including lip whiskers: Ulysses S. Grant, Rutherford B. Hayes, James A. Garfield, and Benjamin Harrison. Since 1913 presidents have been clean-shaven.

Now Polly was . . . where? . . . drinking navy grog with a strange man—although not too strange; they were on first-name terms.

Sunday without Polly was bad enough; Sunday without *The New York Times* was unthinkable. He phoned the drugstore in Pickax with instructions to save a copy. Meanwhile he put the Siamese through their paces with the battered necktie, groomed them until their fur glistened, and read aloud from a book he found on the shelf above the sofa: *Uncle Wiggly's Story Book.* It was copyrighted in 1921 and had the original pen-and-ink sketches and luscious color plates.

He read them the story about a rich cat who rode around in a chauffeured convertible. They listened raptly to the well-bred mewing and purring of the cat, the squeaking of her mousey servants, the yipping of the dogs who chased her up a tree when her car lost a wheel, and the gentlemanly tones of the elderly rabbit in top hat and gloves who came to her rescue.

Then Qwilleran drove to Pickax for his newspaper. On the way back he recognized the pickup ahead of him. He flashed his headlights, passed it and turned off on the shoulder. The truck pulled up behind, and the two drivers jumped out and shook hands. It was Ernie Kemple, retired insurance agent and active volunteer.

"Ernie! I hear you're riding high!"

"Qwill, you don't know what I've been through!" His booming voice had regained its verve. "D'you have time for a cuppa at the Dismal Diner?"

The Dimsdale Diner deserved its nick-name. It was a converted boxcar at a country crossroads, dilapidated inside and out. The coffee was awful. But the weedy parking lot was always full of pick-ups and vans as farmers and business-men dropped in for smokes, snacks, laughs, and shared information. There was a large table at one end where they hung out.

Qwilleran and Kemple sat at the counter and had coffee served in a styrofoam cup and a doughnut served on a paper napkin.

The voices at the big table were lusty:

"Skeeters don't bother me none. It's those blasted ticks!"

"You can say that again! I spend hours pickin' 'em out of my dogs' hair!"

"Who picks 'em outta your hair?"

"I take a turpentine shampoo. Only way to go."

"The trick is to get the danged blood-suckers outa your flesh afore they dig in."

"Yeah, and don't leave the head in, or you're in bad trouble!"

Kemple said to Qwilleran, "Mind if we

take our coffee out to the car? I've got a weak stomach."

In the privacy of the parking lot he told his story. "You remember Vivian took our daughter out west after she was jilted and cracked up. My in-laws have a ranch out there, and we thought she might meet a decent guy. Vivian made several trips out there to check her progress and kept staying longer and longer. I should've smelled a rat! My wife had met another man! . . . Well . . . why fight it? I gave her a divorce and also the million-dollar collection of rare dolls. I'd spent five years researching them in England, Germany, and France."

"But you plunged into the idea of an antique mall," Qwilleran recalled, "and that was good."

"Yep. I found the perfect building in Pickax, made an offer to buy, and signed up dealers for the mall. Then the owner decided to keep the building and steal my idea."

"I remember. It was a shock to all of us."

"I was really down, Qwill. It's a wonder I didn't hit the bottle."

Qwilleran nodded sympathetically. "I've

been there myself. What pulled you through?"

"You won't believe this—and I usually don't tell it—but my father spoke to me! He departed this life twenty years ago, but I remembered something he used to say. If somebody stole my baseball mitt or if I wasn't picked for the first team, he'd say, 'Rise above it, boy. Rise above it.' He was only a potato farmer, but he knew a lot about life, and I'd take his advice. I'd imagine myself in a hot-air balloon, high in the sky, looking down on the scene of my disappointment, which looked pretty insignificant from that altitude. Now I realize that distancing yourself from a problem aids your perspective."

"I'd heard that you were in Florida last winter."

"Yes, the Gulf Coast is very popular with folks around here, and I had the good luck to meet a nice Scottish woman from Black Creek, who owned the flea market. We talked about the new look in Black Creek—and how a first-class antique mall would be more suitable than a flea market. Result: We're in partnership. She works with the dealers; I handle the business end. Grand opening is Saturday. First ad runs Friday. And the Scottish community is giving a preview. . . . Would you like to see how it's shaping up? Dealers are still moving in. You can meet our floor manager, who'll have charge of the daily operation. She says she knows you. Janelle Van Roop."

"Our paths crossed briefly last summer," Qwilleran said, "pleasant young woman." Actually, he was wondering how this sweet, shy, soft-spoken personality, hidden under a mop of very long hair, could manage anything more dynamic than an old ladies' home. He had met her at a residence for the widows of commercial fishermen.

"I'd like to see the facility," he said to Kemple.

He followed the pickup truck to a side street in Black Creek, where a large barn-like building gleamed under a coat of white paint. Painted across the front were the words ANTIQUE VILLAGE. The large double doors were open, and rocking chairs, tables and hutch cabinets were being carried in.

"It's been cleaned up a lot," Kemple said. "We just painted everything white. If you have any suggestions, don't hesitate to make them."

The two long walls were lined with three-sided booths having wall space for wall furniture and hanging objects. Down the center of the hall were larger spaces divided by latticework, designed for free-standing furniture. Kemple said in a low rumble that passed for a whisper, "They pay less per square foot, and it encourages furniture displays. We want to get that kind of reputation—not just a barnful of knickknacks. Some of the large pieces coming in include an Art Deco dining table, an old square piano made into a desk, an eight-foot hutch cupboard, and a carved church pew."

"Mr. Qwilleran!" came a woman's voice, forceful but cordial. "Do you remember me? Janelle—from the Safe Harbor Residence."

"Of course I remember you," he said, concealing his surprise. Two years of college, contact with the workaday world, and a businesslike haircut had given her a managerial briskness that disguised her petite stature.

The boss said, "Janelle, show him around. I have to make a few phone calls."

"Have you seen the recycled furniture?" she asked. "A young man in Sawdust City makes shutters, doors, small windows, railings and mantels into tables, desks, cabinets, chests, and so forth. They're wonderful in beach houses and fun accents anywhere."

The mismatched components of each piece were given a coat of paint to tie everything together. White, terra-cotta and moss green were among the colors the creator had chosen.

"What do you think?" Janelle asked.

"Certainly original. Some are quite witty. They'll appeal to people who don't take themselves too seriously."

From somewhere came an impudent cry, "Cuckoo! Cuckoo!"

"Who said that?" Qwilleran demanded with facetious indignation.

Giggling slightly, she said it was one of

Arnold's clocks. "He has shops in Lock-master and Mooseville, but he likes the idea of having a booth in a mall."

On display in Arnold's booth were brass andirons, cranberry glass candlesticks, Oriental scatter rugs with the mellowness of age, a birdcage made of twigs, framed engravings of Niagara Falls and the Hudson River, several pressed-wood kitchen clocks ticking loudly, and a cuckoo clock like the one Gus Limburger had promised to his handyman.

Across the hall a dealer called for Janelle, and she excused herself to go and help. Qwilleran looked around and was attracted to a locked glass case in which several curiosities were displayed: a pair of bronze monkeys holding stubby candles, a tall brass oil lamp from India, a small pillow covered with a scrap of needlepoint worked with the date, 1847. The item that riveted his attention was a framed oil painting, about twelve by fifteen. It was a beach scene, obviously painted in the twenties, judging from the modest bathing attire.

"What is this display?" he asked Janelle when she returned.

"It's a not-for-sale loan-exhibit. We're having a sign made. The dealers are invited to show their personal treasures. Each one will have a label identifying the item and the owner. The oil painting is mine."

"It has a haunting quality. How do you happen to own it?"

"It's a long story! With kind of a spooky ending."

"I'd like to hear it if you don't mind."

"Oh, I'd love to tell you!" she glanced at the growing activity in the hall.

"When you're not busy," he said quickly, "and when I have my tape recorder."

"I could come in early tomorrow—nine thirty . . ."

"Done deal!" he said, as another dealer cried "Miss Van Roop!"

Kemple came out of the office. "How do you like what you see?"

"So far, so good. What's the platform at the end of the hall?"

"It was used for auctions when the flea market was here, but they've been discontinued. We haven't decided, yet, what to do with it."

"How would you like a loan-exhibit of museum-quality black walnut furniture dated 1900—with a romantic history to boot?"

"Are you kidding me? Or what?"

"It belongs to the K Fund and needs a temporary home until the new museum is built. It's heavily insured, of course."

"I know. Anything the K Fund does is done right. What'll they want from us?"

"Some kind of barrier around the edge of the platform, so the public has no access to the exhibit items."

Kemple said, "Janelle's boyfriend could build one out of old porch railings. He's the guy who builds recycled furniture from bits and pieces of old houses. When would you be moving the stuff in? Maybe we should have an armed guard," he added with a chuckle.

Qwilleran said, "Would you like to hand out leaflets telling the story behind the furniture. There's an element of mystery about the three mirrors, all of which are cracked in the same unusual way."

"This is getting better all the time. Where do we get those?"

"I have all the information," Qwilleran said. "I'll write the copy, and you can have it run off at the quick-print shop in Pickax."

"Wait till my partner hears this!" Kemple said.

Qwilleran returned home in high spirits. He had pulled strings, thrown his weight around, killed two birds with one stone, and told a couple of harmless fibs. By way of celebration he announced "Crabmeat tonight!" as the Siamese met him at the door.

First he called the attorney at home. "Bart, I won't apologize for calling you at home on Sunday, because I know you're eager for this information. The Antique Village that's opening this weekend is a class-act under Ernie Kemple's eagle eye, and they are interested in having our black walnut furniture as a loan-exhibit. We'd better insure it."

"What's its value?"

"Seventy-five thousand at least. It's a

hundred years old, of rare quality, and rich in legend."

"Who can verify that?"

"Susan Exbridge."

Next Qwilleran called the antique dealer at home. "Susan, if Allen Barter calls you about some hundred-year-old black walnut furniture with a red-hot provenance, it's okay to say it's worth seventy-five thousand. I'll explain to you later."

"Anything you say, darling," she purred.

"Have you heard they're going to build a historical museum? I'm sure they'll want you to be on the board of directors."

Finally he called Nick Bamba. "I've found a new home for the black walnut furniture that we moved to Sandpit Road. It will be a loan-exhibit at the Antique Village. They'll be ready for it this week. Can you accommodate them when they call? Eventually it will move to the museum being built—but don't repeat this. It won't be officially announced until the right location is found."

Qwilleran hung up with satisfaction. Starting an unfounded rumor was one of the chief pleasures 400 miles north of everywhere.

At six o'clock he ambled along the creek to Cabin One, where the Underhills were waiting outside Hannah's porch.

"She's putting her face on," Wendy said. "She bought a new pantsuit to wear tonight, and she looks splendiferous!"

Doyle said, "Have you seen our new neighbors in Cabin Four? They claim to be fly-fishermen, and one was fly-casting in the creek this morning, but I think they're cops, working on the Hackett case."

"Here she comes!"

Hannah did indeed look handsome, a far cry from the dumpy, dowdy character in the opera. Her fans applauded and shouted "Bravo! . . . Congratulations! . . . Will you give me an autograph?"

She responded with smiles and admirable poise.

They walked up to the inn with an escort of squirrels, expecting peanuts.

"They multiply like rabbits," Doyle said. "What happens when the inn has ten thousand on the premises?"

"They transport them to Canada," Qwilleran said, "under cover of darkness."

At the inn Cathy Hooper was enjoying her responsibility as interim manager. "Mr. and Mrs. Bamba are in Mooseville," she said, "taking Lovey and Grandma to church and out to Sunday dinner."

Qwilleran's party was seated at his favorite table in the window, and he ordered a bottle of champagne for his guests and a split of "poor man's champagne" for himself (an extra-dry ginger ale). He had also arranged for a floral centerpiece with Hannah's name on the tag. Glasses were raised to Hannah, and compliments flowed like the wine.

Then Qwilleran said, "I have something to report about the video of 'Pirates' that you lent me, Hannah. It has an unusual appeal for my male cat, although he's never attracted to the TV screen unless the programming is about tropical birds. I've played it twice, and both times he's become quite excited."

"Keep it for a while," she said. "Although I enjoyed rehearsing and performing, I'm glad it's over and I can do other things. You don't need to return it until you leave."

Wendy asked, "What other things are you going to do?"

The reply was hesitant. "Well . . . right now I'm concerned about the boy next door. He's awfully neglected and I can't help thinking about my grandson who's his age. I keep some books and games and puzzles for his visits, and I'm going to ask Marge if he can come over for milk and cookies and Chinese checkers."

They placed their orders (roast loin of lamb for the women, lamb shank for the men). Then Qwilleran brought up the subject of the old books in the cabins. "I assume you all have a shelf of popular classics. I suggest an exchange program. I have an *Alice in Wonderland*. Any takers?"

Hannah said, "I could read it to my grandkids when they come visiting."

Doyle said, "If anyone has a *Fanny Hill*, I'll trade two to one."

"Would you settle for *Lolita* in French?" Qwilleran asked.

Wendy asked, "Would anyone like *The*

Picture of Dorian Gray? I think it's by Ogden Nash."

"Oscar Wilde," Qwilleran said. "I'll take it. My favorite is Trollope."

Jules Verne and Henry James went on the block.

The books were forgotten when the entrees were served, but after a while Qwilleran inquired about the Bushland photo show in Pickax.

Doyle said, "That guy has great talent, and he's real down-to-earth. He invited us for a cruise on his boat."

Hannah said, "I know Bushy. He photographed my miniatures. His ancestors were commercial fishermen."

Qwilleran asked Doyle, "Are you satisfied with the wildlife shots you're getting?"

"Well, I'm limited, shooting from the creek. Most species are inland, but Wendy doesn't want me to go into the woods."

"There are bears and wolves in the woods," she said. "And swamps. I don't want him going ashore alone. Anything could happen. He could break a leg, and who would know—"

"I could take a cell phone."

"That would do a lot of good if a black bear came up behind you while you were shooting her cubs. Female bears can be very protective, very savage. You've seen that huge mounted bear at the Black Bear Café! . . . What do you think, Qwill?"

What could he say? "It would seem prudent to have a partner."

Hannah said, "Qwill, do you remember the bears that used to come to the dump in Mooseville? They were a big tourist attraction. But they were feeding the bears, and the wildlife people objected. Then the dump was replaced by a modern disposal system. And the bears disappeared."

Doyle guessed, "Probably sent to zoos around the country."

"I know what happened to them!" Wendy said with her brown eyes flashing. "A friend of mine is a forest ranger. She told me the bears were transported to the Black Forest Conservancy, where they can have a natural diet—and proliferate!!"

"Wendy always overreacts," her husband said.

"He never listens to me! And he knows it stresses me when he takes chances!"

There was a moment of awkward silence until Qwilleran signaled for the plates to be removed and said, "Shall we look at the dessert menu. I recommend the black walnut pie."

Doyle was cool, but Wendy's face was flushed.

"Speaking of pie," Hannah said hastily, "I've been reading nursery rhymes to Danny, and he wanted to know how the blackbirds could sing if they'd been baked in a pie."

That reminded Qwilleran that Danny had come to see if the cats had found their mittens.

There was more uncomfortable small talk while they waited for three orders of pie; Wendy had decided against having dessert. And the festive spirit of the occasion never revived.

They walked back down the hill—Hannah chattering to Doyle, Qwilleran trying to cheer up Wendy—and they forgot to exchange books.

chapter eleven

Early on Monday morning Qwilleran went to the inn for a quick breakfast, taking his review of *Pirates* to be faxed. He also told the Bambas about the plans for the black walnut heirlooms at the Antique Village.

Nick said, "I'll send two guys to Sandpit Road to get them out of hock—right away!"

"Not so fast!" Qwilleran said. "Arrangements have to be made. And when you pick up the stuff, you should be one of the guys. We don't want the cracked mirrors to be shattered. The way they're cracked, they're mysterious; if shattered, they would be just a mess."

"Will we get a credit line for the exhibit?"

"A tasteful card," Qwilleran told him, "will say that the pieces were found in a turret at the Nutcracker Inn, where they had been locked up for a hundred years. It will also be mentioned in the leaflet handed out to visitors."

Lori said, "Qwill, you'd make a wonderful publicity man!"

"Watch your language! To a journalist, them's fighting words."

Janelle was waiting in the office of the Antique Village when Qwilleran arrived with his tape recorder. She poured two cups of coffee. The painting itself had been brought from the display case and was propped on the desk. Briefly he tried to analyze its fascination. Although it had been painted long ago and far away, the people on the beach seemed so real that one was teleported into the scene. Sunning, digging in the sand, and reading all without a beer cooler or topless swimmer.

"Okay, how did you happen to acquire this painting?" he asked Janelle.

"Well," she began, "when I was attending MCCC, a classmate and I went to Chicago on spring break. First time! We gawked at the tall buildings, squealed when we rode the elevated, giggled on escalators, and ate food we'd never heard of before. One day we ventured into a big gallery selling furniture from European castles and paintings as big as billboards. But I saw this little painting among the giants and couldn't stop staring at it. A man was walking around with his hands behind his back, and I asked about it. He said it came in a large shipment and was smaller than they usually handled, but if I liked it I could have it for ten dollars! I felt weak in the knees!"

"Were you able to learn anything about it?"

"A sticker on the back gives 1921 as the date and the name of a gallery in Amsterdam. It's signed, but no one can make out the signature."

It was a beach scene with the ocean in the background and the sand dotted with bathers and some beach chairs made of wicker and hooded for protection against the sun.

Qwilleran said, "I don't see any sun worshippers, any bikinis, any frisbees or any Jet Skis."

A small boy with a tin pail and shovel was sitting on the sand, digging, while a woman bent over him with motherly concern. She was wearing a blue dress with short full skirt and puffed sleeves—the focal point of the artwork—also a cloche hat and knee-high stockings.

Janelle said, "I showed it to some elderly women, and they said that was a *bathing* dress; the cloche was a rubber *bathing* hat; she was wearing *bathing* shoes and *bathing* stockings. That was how she took a dip in the waves. . . . But you haven't heard the best part! I was living at home, and my mother let me hang my treasure in the living room. One day my grandfather visited us. He was born in the Netherlands, and he said, 'I know that beach! I was there when the picture was painted! . . . That's me digging in the sand! The woman in blue was my mother!' Qwill, it gave me shivers! The woman in blue was my great-grandmother! Is that why the painting had such a powerful attraction for me in the gallery?"

"Hmmm," he mused, tamping his moustache. "Amazing coincidence!" He lived with Koko; he knew all about amazing coincidence.

"Cuckoo! Cuckoo!" came a poorly timed comment from the main hall.

"Same to you!" he shouted over his shoulder. "Janelle, thanks for a thought-provoking story. It'll run in my Friday space, and readers can come in to see the painting on Saturday."

Another voice came from the main hall, "Ms. Van! Ms. Van! They spelled my name wrong on my booth!"

Janelle shrugged. Qwilleran saluted and left.

On the way home he stopped at the inn for mail and found two postcards from Polly. The first had a view of an early maritime village—and bad news:

Dear Qwill—Lost one of my good gold earrings! Looked everywhere! Retraced my steps! Can't imagine how it happened. Sprained ankle—nothing serious!

> Love from Polly

Qwilleran could imagine; she had been drinking navy grog; rum was not her drink. . . . The second card, mailed the next day, came from Sturbridge Village, showing a white colonial house with a horse and carriage at the door.

> Dear Qwill—Delightful place! I could spend a week here! So peaceful! Picturesque farmhouses, meadows, split-rail fences. Walter found my earring!
>
> Love from Polly

Qwilleran wondered why she had not mentioned *where* Walter found the earring. But he had other matters on his mind, such as what to write for the "Qwill Pen" column the next day. He thought he could write a thousand words on "Whiskers in the White House" . . . who, when and why . . . to shave or not to shave . . . the connection between war and facial hair . . . political influences . . .

He carried his typewriter to the porch and had inserted a sheet of paper when Yum Yum leaped up and landed like a feather, purring throatily. She was in one of her amorous moods, having followed him around and rubbed his ankles ever since he returned. Now she was going to monitor his typing, listening to the click of the keys, watching the carriage travel slowly across and then jerk back.

Half in kindliness and half in self-defense, he picked her up and walked back and forth, massaging her ears, nuzzling the back of her neck with his chin, whispering sweet words that he would not wish to have quoted. With a sudden grunt she jumped to the floor, walked to the kitchen for a drink of water, then settled down for a nap on the blue cushion. "Cats!" Qwilleran muttered as he returned to his typing. The click of keys resounded across the water, and a passing canoeist yelled a greeting. It was Doyle, going up the creek to disappear in a swamp, or be bitten by a rabid fox, or get clobbered by a bear, or suffer some other fate that his wife feared.

Soon after, Wendy herself came along the footpath, carrying books. She was not walking joyously as usual, but trudging.

He went out to meet her, and she held up two slim volumes. "I found some Trollope for you, Qwill. In the library at the inn. They said it was all right to take them."

"That was very thoughtful of you. Will you come on the porch for a drink of fruit juice?"

"Nothing to drink, thanks, but I'd like to talk to you." Her eyes had lost their sparkle. "I just came to apologize for the way Doyle and I argued at dinner last night."

"Think nothing of it, Wendy. We all get hot under the collar once in a while."

"What do you think about the danger in the woods?"

He had heard about poisonous snakes in the bogs and deer-ticks dropping off the trees, but—"You mentioned a friend who's a forest ranger. Is she one of Dr. Abernethy's daughters, by any chance?"

"Yes, I knew her in college, and it was her raving about Moose County that brought us up here—the natural beauty, the perfect summer weather, the slow pace—"

"But nothing about danger in the woods?"

"It wasn't an issue. I didn't know Doyle would be so determined to photograph bear cubs. . . . The trouble is, Qwill, I'm a worrier! I worry about my husband's safety! You can't tell a worrier to—just—stop—worrying. . . . We've been married only two years. We have plans for a family and a wonderful future! And to complicate matters, I'm supposed to avoid stress. I practice the rules of health and tranquillity, but then . . . something like this comes along, and I worry!"

Qwilleran was nodding and looking sympathetic and wondering what he could say.

"Well, if only you could say something to him! He'd listen to you! He has a lot of respect for you. And you live here . . ."

He was thinking fast; the obvious solution to a problem is not always the best. "I understand your distress, Wendy, and you have my utmost sympathy. I want to help, but there's a wrong approach and a right approach. I need to think about it . . . and I will think about it . . ."

"I'd be so grateful!" She stood up. "You're working. I'll go home."

He walked with her to the water's edge. "I'll be in touch. Thank you for the books."

The titles were *He Knew He Was Right* and *The Eustace Diamonds.* Two of his favorites.

First he made some coffee and then lounged on a porch chair with his feet up. Koko hopped onto the foot of the lounge and sat tall in a businesslike way, his blue eyes brimming with helpfulness, as if he sensed a problem was being solved. The trick, Qwilleran decided, is to involve Doyle in something more interesting than Wendy's Valley of Death. If nothing else, it would provide more time to study the problem. It could be something to flatter the photographer's ego, or fulfill his primal urge to take pictures, or the fun of taking an assignment for the picture page of a small-town newspaper.

Qwilleran made three phone calls: to the managing editor, who had gone to the dentist; to the attorney, who was in conference with a client; to Bushland, who was out on assignment. He left urgent messages with all three.

Barter was the first to respond, and he listened to the proposition with keen interest.

"Did you see the opening of Bushy's exhibit yesterday? Big crowd! And I happen to know there was an editor from a prominent publisher of art books there! We've been talking about having the K Fund publish his landscapes, and we'd better act quickly before he signs with another publisher . . . Also, we have a noted photographer of wildlife vacationing here and doing some extensive shooting. We should grab him, and do a large-format hardcover art book titled *The Beauty of Moose County* as photographed by Bushland and Underhill."

"Great idea! I'm all for it."

"My point is that we should get them under contract fast, before this other publisher swoops in."

"How fast?"

"Frankly, Bart, I think it would be to our advantage if you could fly the two guys to

Chicago and back on the shuttle Wednesday."

"No reason why we couldn't. I'll make the appointment and plane reservations, if you'll alert the photographers."

"Be happy to do that. Both of them should have samples of their work to show, by the way."

Qwilleran had never actually seen any of Doyle's work; all his exposed film would be taken home to Cleveland for developing. Still, it was good enough for a cover on the *Smithsonian*—that is, if it happened to be true. Young photographers had been known to boast.

By the time Bushland phoned, the Scheme was working, and it was all legitimate. There was nothing wrong with a little persuasive hyperbole and truth telling before the fact. They were techniques he had used often during his career.

When Bushy finally called, Qwilleran said, "There's a wildlife photographer here from Down Below, who's been doing a lot of shooting, and the K Fund wants to publish a large-format, hardcover art book featuring your landscapes and his wildlife, to be titled *The Beauty of Moose County.* For laughs we might include a full-page, full-color portrait of a thick, toasty, brown pasty."

"No kidding!" Bushy said. "This is the best thing that's happened to me since the helicopter rescued you, me and Roger from Three Tree Island!"

"It means moving fast, for various reasons. Our legal rep wants to fly you two guys to Chicago to sign contracts and show samples—on Wednesday. The hitch is that none of the wildlife stuff has been developed. Could he use the darkroom at the art center tomorrow?"

"Sure thing! Tell him to call the manager and say I okayed it."

There was more. Bushy had met Doyle and his wife at the photo show—nice couple. Doyle had good credentials; no, Bushy couldn't remember seeing the *Smithsonian* cover.

After that, Qwilleran returned to the porch to type his treatise on presidential whiskers, suggesting a nationwide poll of voters. Did they want their chief executive officer (a) clean-shaven, (b) with long sideburns, (c) with small neat moustache, (d) or other. Readers considered summer the silly season in the "Qwill Pen" column and gladly encouraged the silliness.

Although Qwilleran kept an eye on the creek for Doyle's return, there was no sign of the yellow canoe. It would be ironic, he thought, if this were the day that Wendy's fears were realized. But eventually the sleek craft glided downstream, and soon Doyle was walking back from the boat shed and Koko was announcing him as a trespasser.

Qwilleran went out to meet him. "How was the shoot today?"

"I got some great shots!" the photographer said.

Qwilleran recited his piece: K Fund art book—Bushland and Underhill—day-trip to Chicago to sign contracts—appointment set for Wednesday. "Sorry it's such short notice," Qwilleran said.

"No problem."

"They'll want to see samples. If you can develop and print tomorrow, the dark room at the art center is available."

"No problem."

Later, when Qwilleran dined alone at the inn, he recalled his conversation with Doyle, who had said, "I also caught a skunk in a more-or-less comic situation—and some young foxes. But don't tell Wendy; she'll know I went into the woods. I'm afraid she made a scene at dinner last night. She gets upset over little things."

As Qwilleran chewed his steak reflectively, he compared the two photographers. Bushy, whose talent bordered on genius, was as excited as a little kid over the prospect of signing a contract for an art book. Doyle reacted with a cool "No problem."

Qwilleran could only hope that the owl and the skunk and the young foxes were as good as the photographer thought.

When he returned to the creek, he had half a sourdough roll in his pocket for the ducks. He was pinching off morsels for the hungry flock when a pleasant voice called to him from the porch of Cabin One. Hannah was inviting him to have a glass of iced tea. Although already coffee-logged, he accepted.

"I can't tell you what a wonderful time I

had last night, Qwill! You're such a gracious host." There was a half-finished jigsaw puzzle on the table, and she swept it into a box, explaining, "Danny was here this afternoon. I must tell you, Qwill . . . This morning I went next door and told Marge that I was lonesome for my grandson and I wished Danny could visit me for story-telling and games for a little while each day. She hesitated and then said yes. So this afternoon he came over, and we had a wonderful time. I taught him to sing 'I'm a little teapot, short and stout; / Here's my handle and here's my spout.' And I saw that boy laugh for the first time. Then I taught him how to say 'please' and 'thank you.' He's had no upbringing and certainly not much family life. And he has only one tired white T-shirt. I gave him one that my grandson left here—blue, with a pocket, and he's so thrilled with that pocket! He's never had a shirt with a pocket."

"Excuse me for changing the subject, Hannah, but what's that on your ring finger?"

She blushed and said, "You didn't meet

Uncle Louie, our choral director, did you? We've been getting kind of interested in each other—he's a widower—and today he took me to lunch and gave me this!"

"Well! Best wishes to you both."

"And he told me to ask you something. He wants to compose a comic opera—sort of a parody of Gilbert and Sullivan—and he wonders if you'd write the libretto."

Qwilleran stood up to leave. "Only if Koko can play the lead."

Walking home along the creek and approaching Cabin Three, he noticed that the Underhill car was not there. That meant, probably, that Doyle had taken Wendy out to celebrate. Wrong! She came flying off the screened porch.

"Oh, Qwill! Thank you so much for what you've done! Doyle went to the art center to get a head start on the developing. There's so much to do."

"Don't thank me," he said. "The art book is only a good idea whose time has come."

chapter twelve

Whiskers tickling the nose and a soft paw patting the eyelid could do it every time—quickly, quietly, efficiently. Qwilleran awoke with a start on Tuesday morning, as two furry bodies leaped from his bunk and headed for the kitchen. Despite the rude awakening he was in a good mood—still elated after Monday's successes, still sharing the excitement of two young photographers about to publish their first book. He remembered his own first book, *City of Brotherly Crime.* It was completely forgotten now, and he was lucky to have salvaged a single copy, thanks to the late Eddington Smith.

It occurred to him momentarily that Doyle's photos might not compare favorably with Bushy's superb landscapes. That was a chance they were taking. An owl is an owl is an owl; there is always something noble about an eight-point buck and something comic about a skunk. Such thoughts were interrupted by a call from the attorney.

Barter said, "I've lined up the K Fund boys in Chicago, but the appointment will have to be Thursday, not Wednesday."

"That's all right. It will give Doyle an extra day to prepare his samples."

"Will you write a preface to the book, Qwill?"

"By all means. And I'll volunteer to write the cutlines." Whatever Doyle's wildlife shots lacked in originality, a skillful cutline could cover up with words.

He took his typewriter to the screened porch to work on his Tuesday column, and Koko was sitting alongside the machine, observing the operation—until a sudden sound or scent made his head jerk to the south and his whiskers bristle: Trespasser approaching!

It was Wendy, carrying a white bakery box. "Come in," Qwilleran called to her.

"What are you carrying so carefully? Koko thought it was a bomb."

She said, "Doyle went to the art center, and Hannah and I drove to Fishport for some of those sweet rolls you like. You can keep them in the freezer—just a little thank-you for making things happen." Her eyes were shining, and she bubbled with enthusiasm. "You know, Qwill, I've been so worried about Doyle that I haven't been able to work on my family history, but suddenly I feel inspired again."

"You never told me what inspired you in the first place. You said it was a dramatic incident." Qwilleran sensed fodder for the ever-hungry space on page two. "I'd like to tape it."

The tape recorder was set up on the snack table, and the following interview was later transcribed:

> *What prompted you to write a romantic family history instead of a genealogical chart?*
>
> I couldn't see myself trekking to county courthouses around the country and

searching for births and deaths and mar-
riages. But I loved the stories my great-
aunt told about our family, going back to
about 1800. When she died, she left a
trunkful of old personal correspondence
that none of the cousins wanted, so my
mother took it and stashed it away in the
attic.

Then one day my husband and I were
driving through the Ohio countryside, and
we came to an intersection where a farm
was being cleared for a strip mall. The sign
said there would be a full-service gas station, two fast food places, a laundromat
and a video store. The outbuildings were
already knocked down, and they were
working on the farmhouse itself—a large,
plain two-story colonial. The front door
had been removed, and the sash had disappeared from the windows. It had a
ghostly look. But something caused me to
shout "Stop! Stop!" I wasn't yelling at the
wreckers; I was telling my husband to stop
the car.

We parked on the shoulder, and I saw a
heartrending sight. A dump truck was
backed up to the end of the building, and

another was standing by. They had put a chute in an upstairs window and were throwing personal belongings into the dump truck: clothing, hats, shoes, underwear, stockings, cosmetics, hair brushes, framed photos, books, towels, bedding, lamps, a small radio, and then . . . a cardboard hatbox! Its cover fell off, and hundreds of letters flew out. The breeze scattered them all over the muddy lot.

I'd been controlling my horror and tears, but I broke down when I saw those letters in the mud. Doyle thought I was crazy. I didn't know who had lived there, worn those clothes, read those books, saved those letters, but I cried my eyes out!

That's when I took over my great-aunt's trunkful of correspondence. I'm reading and cataloguing every one: date, names and addresses of senders and recipients, and type of content.

Organizing all this material into a cohesive history sounds like a huge undertaking.

It's a challenge. First I'm absorbing all the events and emotions. Then I'll decide whether to make it the story of a real family . . . or fictionalize it.

But first . . . I'm overwhelmed with the joys and sorrows, successes and failures, pioneer struggles to make a life, and crushing disasters. Those people even found humor in everyday life: an uncle being chased by a bull; a cousin marooned in a tree all night; an aunt ruining the stew when the preacher was coming to dinner.

Do you find the handwriting legible?

More so than my own! Penmanship was important in those days. They dipped a pen in ink and wrote slowly and carefully. Also, letters were formal and sometimes poetic.

When I get home, I'll photocopy a couple of letters, Qwill, and send them to you.

After the tape recorder had been turned off, and Wendy had been complimented on a well-told tale, she said, "I phoned my mother in Cleveland last night while Doyle was at the art center. She knows about my compulsion to worry, and she approved your strategy to divert Doyle's attention from forays into the woods. But when he returns from Chicago—then what? She suggested that we leave here this weekend and spend a few days at the Grand Hotel on Mackinac Island—a kind of second honeymoon, and a kind of second wedding present from her and Dad."

"A splendid idea," Qwilleran said, "although we'll miss you both."

He took his Tuesday copy to the inn to be faxed before the noon deadline, and Lori gave him another picture postcard. It was another view of Sturbridge Village.

> Dear Qwill—Love this place. Bought lots of things to ship home. Mona having reaction to allergy medication. If she flies home, I'll turn in our rental car and travel with Walter.
>
> Love from Polly

Interesting development, he thought. Not once had she said, "Wish you were here."

"Everything okay?" Lori asked.

"Everything's fine."

"We're losing the Underhills."

"Too bad. Nice couple."

"Why can't we have more Underhills and fewer Truffles?"

In the foyer, a new exhibit was being set up in the display case. Susan Exbridge, the antiques dealer, was officiating. It was an assortment of wood carvings, bowls, metal sculptures of animals and what looked like instruments of torture. A sign in the case described it as THE NUTCRACKER INN'S COLLECTION OF NUTCRACKERS.

"Qwill darling!" Susan exclaimed in her histrionic manner. "How do you like it?"

"They must have had a lot of nuts in those days."

"Nuts were a staple food of early American settlers," she said.

"I thought they just bashed them between a rock and a hard place."

"In the late eighteenth century the ritualistic ending to a meal was nuts, and artists and inventors vied to design clever nutcrackers . . . But I can't talk now. Phone me at the shop, darling!"

She left, and Cathy Hooper stepped up. "Don't forget the preview of the reenactment tonight, Mr. Qwilleran. Eight o'clock."

"I've already reserved a booth, Cathy, but thanks for the reminder."

Qwilleran had asked Riker, "Will you and your lovely wife be my guests at a preview of the Saturday Night Brawl?"

And Arch countered, "Will you and your voracious appetite be our guests beforehand?"

No one ever declined a dinner invitation from the food editor.

The Rikers spent summers in a little yellow beach house atop a sand dune overlooking the lake. It was only a thirty-minute commute to the office, but the psychological distance equaled the hundred miles of lake they viewed from their deck.

They were sitting there with apéritifs when Qwilleran arrived, asking, "What happened to the Dunfield house?"

The casual redwood next door had been

replaced by a crisp cube of white stucco and plate glass.

Riker explained, "The widow couldn't sell it or rent it, because of the rumor that it was haunted. So she tore it down and sold the land. Vacant lake frontage is worth more than the same property with an old house on it. What do you think of the new one? Looks like an ice cube. The dune dwellers haven't decided whether it makes us look like a slum—or we make it look ridiculous."

"Who lives there?" Qwilleran was sure he knew the answer.

Mildred said, "A woman from Down Below. I went over to welcome her to the neighborhood, but really to satisfy my curiosity, and she was as friendly as a cold fish. All she could do was complain—about the noise of the surf and the seagulls, about people walking on the beach and staring at her house and even taking snapshots of it, about dead fish washing up. Just to be devilish, I told her not to be alarmed by green lights flashing over the lake at night; they're only UFOs."

Qwilleran said, "She sounds like the

charmer who was staying at the Nut-cracker Inn. Keep Toulouse indoors. She hates cats."

Toulouse was lounging on the railing of the deck with the assurance of a cat who has adopted a food editor. Mildred gave him a morsel of crabmeat as she passed a plate of canapés. "Is it true," she asked, "that household pets are going to be the theme of your next limerick contest?"

"I think so. Rhymes about pets can be fun to write—whimsical, exaggerated, nonsensical. Give me another of those crabmeat things, and I'll show you what I mean."

In the time it took to eat a canapé, Qwilleran produced the following: "A black-and-white stray named Toulouse / found a home in the county of Moose. / He lives on ice cream / and chicken supreme / and crabmeat and paté of goose."

"Hit the nail on the head," Arch said.

Dinner was served al fresco, starting with cold purée of zucchini garnished with fresh blueberries.

Arch said, "Millie throws a handful of blueberries into everything."

"They're good for you," she said.

Then individual beef potpies were served, and Arch remarked, "Do you realize that Millie is descended from a lumber camp cook?"

"My great-grandfather," she said proudly. "The loggers lived on beans and salt pork, hardtack, boiled turnips, and tea boiled with molasses."

"What about flapjacks? I thought they ate stacks of twelve, big as a dinner plate," Qwilleran said.

Arch said, "That sounds like the figment of a Hollywood script writer's imagination."

Because there was no time for a formal dessert, Mildred served coffee and a confection called a Black Walnut Bombshell. They were balls an inch in diameter: buttery, nutty, not too sweet, and tasting faintly of chocolate. She packed some for her guest to take home.

"By the way," Qwilleran said, "did I tell you I'm invited to be guest-of-honor at an MCCC luncheon?"

"What happened?" Arch said wryly. "Did those academic types suddenly find out we have a writer who doesn't do double negatives and dangling adverbs?"

There had been a lack of rapport between the college and the media. Most of the faculty were from Down Below, and many of them commuted.

Qwilleran explained the breakthrough: "I was interviewing Dr. and Mrs. Abernethy, and she seems to have some connection with MCCC. She invited me to the luncheon. There'll be a speaker from Down Below, but they'll introduce me and I'll be expected to say something trenchant in twenty-five words or less."

"Write a limerick," Mildred suggested.

He said, "Do you know that last year's winner in the limerick contest now hangs in the lobby of the Hotel Booze—enlarged and framed? 'There was a young lady in Brrr / who always went swimming in fur. / One day, on a dare, / she swam in the bare / and that was the end of HER.'"

They rode to the Hotel Booze in separate vehicles, so that Qwilleran could search for column material after the performance.

The route lay along the lakeshore to the town of Brrr (as in "cold").

The Black Bear Café occupied half the main floor and was the scene of the reenactment. Qwilleran and his guests were ushered to one of the booths lining three walls. On the other long wall was a bar with twenty stools, and in the center of the room were chairs still upended on tables after the last floor sweeping.

Beverages were being served until eight o'clock, and hotelkeeper Gary Pratt made the rounds of the booths, welcoming the spectators and reminding them to look at the programs on their tables. With his shambling gait and shaggy black beard and hair, he looked as ursine as the eight-foot mounted bear at the entrance.

The programs credited Roger Mac-Gillivray, historian and coach; Carol and Larry Lanspeak, directors; Thornton Haggis, stage manager, who also played the role of "Whitey."

Principals were Whitey, the saloon-keeper; Jake, his helper; Mrs. Watts and Lucy, barmaids; and George, the most-favored customer. Then there were lumberjacks, just in from the backwoods camps; the elite river-drivers from French Canada; sawyers from the mills at the river's mouth; dance hall girls; and sailors from the schooners in the harbor.

Mildred, a native of the area, knew them all. "Lucy" was the daughter of her hairdresser; "Jake" taught math at the high school and coached the wrestling team; "Stinko" worked at Toodles' supermarket; "George" was an insurance agent.

At eight o'clock the lights blinked for attention, and then blacked out, leaving only the vigil candles in the booths. The audience was silent, but a commotion could be heard beyond the entrance doors at the far right end of the bar. At the opposite end a double door opened and in came Whitey with his bar apron tied around his middle and with his shock of white hair looking like a torch in the grubby saloon. His helper, Jake, followed—a mountain of a man in a plaid flannel shirt. The two barmaids, one middle-aged and one young, wore long gray granny dresses with small white collars and white ruffled caps.

Jake went to work, setting up the chairs

around the tables, while the barmaids wiped the tabletops. Whitey started pouring stage whiskey (cold tea) from whiskey bottles into shot glasses.

There were impatient thumps on the entrance door and shouts of "Open up!" Whitey consulted a large gold watch on a long chain and gave a nod to his helper. After unlocking the doors, Jake barred the entrance with his huge arms and admitted the thirsty horde in a thin trickle while bellowing, "No corks! No corks!"

He referred to the caulks, or steel pins, that could be attached to boots for gripping logs. Indoors, they damaged floors. In a violent fight, they damaged flesh.

In they came! Husky lumberjacks in beards and pigtails and burly backwoods clothing . . . Sailors of a taut, wiry build, wearing striped jerseys, tight pants, and hats with brims turned up all around. They yelled with the exuberance of youth:

"Whitey, y'ol' galoot! Ain't you dead yet?"

"Pour the red-eye, Whitey! I gotta thirst that'd drain a swamp!"

"Where's George? He owes me a drink!"

"Ain't George here yet?"

The loggers dropped into chairs around the tables and got out the cards and dice. The sailors kept their distance from this rough crowd and lined up at the bar. Also at the bar were three of the elite river-drivers in red caps and red sashes, just arrived from Quebec to ride the logs downstream like daredevils. A few dance hall girls, swishing their short skirts and twitching their bare shoulders, were especially interested in the French-Canadians.

The barmaids were bustling about the tables when young Lucy shrieked, "He pinched me!"

"Slap his face!" Mrs. Watts shouted, but before Lucy could summon the nerve, big Jake was on the spot. He raised the culprit by the collar, glared menacingly in his face, then dropped him back into his seat.

"Yahoo!" the other loggers yelled. In Whitey's saloon it was all right to flirt with the dance hall girls but not with the hired help.

Whitey signaled to three sailors, and they put their heads together and sang sea shanties in three-part harmony. "Blow the man down, bullies, blow the man down," and then the rollicking "What do you do with a drunken sailor early in the morning?"

Meanwhile the card players were gambling noisily for pennies; the crap-shooters were yelling incantations to the dice; the bawdy joke tellers were putting their heads together and then exploding in obscene laughter.

Next, three girls perched on barstools, crossed their knees and sang "She's only a bird in a gilded cage," while the patrons yelled, "Ain't the one in the middle a dinger! Chip chip chip!"

One quiet logger who was not a part of the raucous group tried to join one of the groups around the tables. He was shooed away, and someone shouted, "Vamoose, Stinko." Wandering over to the bar, he was rebuffed again, and one of the river-drivers barked, "Casse-toi, Bouc Puant!" Whitey sent him to sit at the end of the bar and told Lucy to take him a drink. Sitting there alone, Stinko pulled a mouth-organ from his pocket and entertained himself with simple tunes.

It was a lively Saturday night at the Hotel Booze. Two lumberjacks sang several verses about "the frozen logger who stirred his coffee with his thumb." Two sailors walked around the room on their hands, and one of them did cartwheels the length of the bar top, while barflies yelped and grabbed their drinks. "How about pourin' some more eagle-sweat, Whitey?"

At the card table, tempers were flaring. "You cheatin' hell-pup!" Fists started to swing. Immediately Jake was on the scene, collaring the two rowdies, one in each hand and giving them the bum's rush out the side door, leading to the alley. He returned brushing the dust off his hands, and Whitey signaled to the trio of sailors, who sang, "Michael, row the boat ashore, hallelujah!" Quietly the evicted pair sneaked back into the saloon, one of them holding a red-stained rag to his nose and acting as a crutch for the other, who was limping.

"Whitey!" someone shouted. "Why ain't George here? Has he gone to get his teeth fixed?"

"George won't be comin' here any

more," said the saloonkeeper. "He got in a fight Thursday night and was sluiced."

"Sluiced! Holy Mackinaw! Where've they got 'im?"

"In Pete's funeral parlor next door. Can't bury him till Monday. They've got him on ice. Pete built him a pine box, but George didn't have money for a headstone, so we're taking up a collection." Whitey put a tin cup on the bar and rattled the coins in it. One by one the mourners filed past and dropped a few pennies in the cup.

Then a lumberjack yelled, "Let's go and get 'im! Let's bring ol' George back for one last drink together!"

"Yahoo!" Six volunteers bolted out the side door, while Whitey and the barmaids poured and served, and the customers cheered and stamped their boots.

Soon there was kicking at the alley entrance, and Jake opened the double doors to admit the pallbearers with a six-foot pine box. The roomful of rowdies was strangely silent.

The pallbearers shouted, "Move three stools away! . . . Gotta prop 'im up! . . . Lean the box against the bar! . . . Whitey,

got a crowbar? . . . Hang onto the box. . . .
Keep it upright!"

With the wrenching sound of boards and
nails, the lid of the coffin came off, and the
audience gasped. There was George—
stiff, chalk-faced, still in his bloody clothing.

Two gunshots shattered the breathless
quiet! And the lights went out.

The room was in darkness only long
enough for the reenactors—including the
white-faced George—to line up, facing the
audience, who responded with whoops,
cheers, applause, whistles and yahoos.

The Rikers had to leave, but
Qwilleran and most of the others attending the preview mingled with the players and congratulated them.

Whitey explained, "This is a reenactment
of a true incident that took place right here
in the Hotel Booze. His name wasn't
George. We don't know what his name
was or which of the headstones in the old
loggers' cemetery is his. My great-grand-

father was a stonecutter, and the story has been handed down in our family."

Qwilleran singled out Stinko for congratulations and questions. "Whose idea was it to have a character with a B.O. problem?"

"It was Roger's idea," was the answer, "but I volunteered. It gave me a chance to do a little character acting and play my harmonica. They say the stench in lumber camps was horrendous: Forty men sleeping in one big shanty, drying their snow-soaked socks around a pot-bellied stove, with no facilities for washing up. Phooey!"

Qwilleran handed out compliments: To Jake for his strong-arm act; to the river-driver for his French accent; to the girls for their provocative maneuvers. He learned that the singing sailors came from the chorus of *Pirates of Penzance,* and the acrobats were high school gymnasts.

Jake said to him, "Have you heard anything about a movie being made in Moose County—about the logging era?"

"Not a word! Where did you hear it?" As a journalist Qwilleran hated being in the dark—about anything.

"Well, I'm working at my father's gas station this summer, and a guy with an out-of-state license said he was an advance man, lining up muscle-men as extras in a lumberjack film. He told me to keep it under my hat because another film producer had the same idea, and they wanted to beat the competition."

"Hollywood epic or independent documentary?"

"He didn't say, and I didn't ask, because I wasn't interested. I have this job with my dad and a commitment to the reenactors, plus I'm gonna be a father in August! First time!"

"Congratulations!"

"Thanks. It's exciting, all right! And terrifying, in a way." Jake grinned sheepishly.

Qwilleran said, "The producers won't have trouble finding their extras. There are more Paul Bunyans per acre in Moose County than in any other place I've known!"

"My dad says we're descended from Vikings. He tells some good stories."

Qwilleran drove home in good spirits. Good show! Good dinner! And a few leads for the "Qwill Pen" column and *Short & Tall Tales.*

The Siamese were waiting with loud vocal complaints and irritably jerking tails that seemed to say, You're late! . . . Where've you been? . . . Where's our stuff?

"You missed a good show tonight," Qwilleran told them as he prepared their bedtime treat. He himself had a cup of coffee and a black walnut bombshell from the supply Mildred had given him. Polly would disapprove; too many calories. Where was Polly tonight? He wondered.

He had another bombshell.

chapter thirteen

Wednesday dawned bright and full of promise in Cabin Five. Qwilleran had enjoyed the Saturday Night Brawl, and the melodies of sea shanties were running through his mind. His respite in Black Creek had been satisfying, as respites go. He had found leads for his column, met people, solved their problems, and learned something—about squirrels and black walnut trees. Soon Polly would be coming home—maybe. She might decide to detour through Ohio.

As he opened a can of Extra Fancy Crabmeat, he said to the Siamese, "You deserve this! You've been a couple of good eggs the last ten days." They watched him attentively, their tails gently lapping the floor, until . . . with a convulsive movement, Koko whirled about and dashed for the screened porch. His sudden action was enough to make Qwilleran drop the can opener and follow.

What he saw was a yellow canoe gliding upstream with Doyle at the paddle, making purposeful strokes. The photographer was supposed to be in the darkroom at the art center, processing film for the art book! With a shrug Qwilleran finished feeding the cats and had one of Wendy's sweet rolls for his own breakfast.

While sitting on the porch with his second cup of coffee, he felt a certain sensation in his left temple and realized that Koko was staring at him. If the cat was up to his old trick of thought-transference, why couldn't he be more specific? Qwilleran had an uneasy feeling that he had forgotten something . . .

Suddenly he catapulted out of his chair and went to the typewriter. He had forgotten to write a short piece about the furniture locked up in the tower; it was supposed to be a handout at the Antique Village on Friday night! Drawing on "The Legend of the Rubbish Heap," and the condition of the furniture, and his own imagination, he wrote "The Mystery of the Three Cracked Mirrors."

More than a century before the Age of Computer Millionaires, fortunes were made on the American frontier by hard-working, risk-taking pioneers. One such entrepreneur built a splendid brick mansion in Black Creek, using local black walnut for interior woodwork and furniture. He had two sons, but his daughter Elsa was his pet. For her he arranged a good marriage into an important family and planned a wedding that was the talk of the county.

On the very eve of the nuptials, however, Elsa eloped with the man she really loved, who happened to be the son of her father's worst enemy. This was 1900, understand, when grown daughters were expected to obey their parents, no matter what! In fury her father pronounced a solemn curse on Elsa and defaced the black walnut furniture that had been made for her bridal suite. Clenching the fist that wore a large gold signet ring, he smashed it against three mirrors. For a hundred years these damaged goods have been locked up in the mansion that is now the Nutcracker Inn.

Sad to say, Elsa and her true love were among the casualties of the Great San Francisco Earthquake of 1906.

Without picking up his daily postcard, Qwilleran went to the Antique Village. He chose to bike on his Silverlight; he had had too little exercise on this trip. Playing the necktie game with the Siamese didn't count.

He was braking at the front door, when a booming voice across the street said, "Hey, Qwill! You look good in that helmet! You should wear it all the time!"

Ernie Kemple was carrying a spinning wheel into the building. Qwilleran said, "I'll hold the door for you, if you'll let me park my Silverlight in the office."

Inside, dealers were bustling about; Janelle was trying to be everywhere at once; a pleasant woman was introduced as Mrs. Munroe, Ernie's partner; and the man who built recycled furniture had found a stone balustrade to protect the exhibit platform.

Qwilleran said, "I'm a little late with this copy for your handout, but the print shop in Pickax will give you one-day service."

"I'll take it down there right away."

"Better read it first."

"Better yet, I'll round up the girls, and you can read it to us."

The two assistants reported to the office, and Qwilleran read the story of the millionaire pioneer, his daughter Elsa, the marriage he arranged for her, Elsa's elopement with the son of her father's worst enemy— and the disastrous conclusion. Janelle dabbed her eyes; Mrs. Munroe gulped a few times; Ernie shook his head sadly no doubt thinking of his own daughter . . . Then he took the copy and left for Pickax.

Qwilleran used the phone to make arrangements for delivering the historic furniture, then said he would like to browse around for awhile. One booth had a cross-cut saw six feet long, with a handle on each end and murderous two-inch teeth. A similar one had hung on the wall in the log cabin he inherited, but it looked too threatening; he had disposed of it.

The dealer said, "This saw represents

the early history of Moose County. With a Paul Bunyan on each end of it, who knows how many million trees it cut down? I can close my eyes and hear the rhythmic grinding of those sharp teeth through the trunk of a great oak! It was a sign of man's determination to make a life for himself and his family! . . . Today I hear the whine of a chain saw, and it chills my blood. Another nail in the coffin of Planet Earth!"

"Cuckoo! Cuckoo!" That bird was always butting into every conversation, but it reminded Qwilleran it was time to go home for lunch. He asked the dealer for his card.

By the time he showered and dressed and walked up the hill to the inn, it was two o'clock. Nick handed him a postcard and said, "We're moving the furniture tonight. I'm going along to make sure they baby it."

The picture on the card was that of Independence Hall, and Qwilleran wondered, What's she doing in Philadelphia? But after he was seated at a table, where he could read the fine print, he realized that it was the Henry Ford Museum in Dearborn, Michigan.

> Dear Qwill—What a museum! Everything from Georgian silver to locomotives! Miles of aisles! I'm doing it in a wheelchair. Walter sends regards.
>
> Love, Polly

"Same to you, Walter old boy," he said to the postcard.

In the foyer a signboard announcing coming events reminded him that the MCCC luncheon was scheduled for the next day. He had considered a limerick, as suggested by Mildred, with rhymes like academic, polemic, endemic, systemic—but found them too stuffy.

He took a window table in the dining room and watched the squirrels flicking their tails in a secret language; no wonder they were called flickertails in some parts of the country. As he waited for his ham and eggs, he formulated his plans:

He would ask the management to put a bag of peanuts at each place—with his business card, which read "Straight from the Qwill Pen" and, in smaller print, "Every Tuesday and Friday in the *Moose County Something.*" When introduced at the luncheon, he would explain, soberly, that the goobers ushered in the annual "nutty season" in the "Qwill Pen" column. The kick-off would be a limerick contest, the nuttier the better. He would recite an example: "Our squirrels are as smart as can be / Alumni of MCCC / They went to college / in search of knowledge / and to learn how to run up a tree." Then he would sit down, amid laughter and thunderous applause— or grim silence, as the case might be.

He enjoyed the ham and eggs and had three cups of coffee and walked down the hill with satisfaction, unaware of the complications that awaited him.

When he reached the creek there was singing and childish laughter coming from Cabin One.

Cabin Two was dark and silent except for a flickering blue light and the senseless noise of a television set that no one is watching.

There was no music coming from Cabin Three, but Wendy came off the porch to greet him, though not with any enthusiasm. "How's everything going?" he asked. "Did you get your reservations at the Grand Hotel?"

She nodded absently and looked at her watch. "My mother arranged it."

"Did Doyle finish his printing for the Chicago junket?"

"Not quite. He's supposed to meet Bushy at the photo lab at five o'clock to coordinate their samples. Meanwhile, as you can guess, he's gone canoeing. I slept late, and he left me a note."

"Did he take his camera?"

She gave a humorless laugh. "Of course! Just in case something special swims by or flies over. But he promised he wouldn't go into the woods."

"Good!" Qwilleran murmured without conviction. "Don't leave without giving me your home address; I'll send you tearsheets of the dump-truck story."

Two gunshots shattered the quiet. "What's that?" Wendy asked sharply.

"Rabbit hunters. Some local families live on rabbit meat; it's all they can afford."

She kept looking at her watch. "What time do you have?" she asked finally.

"Three-forty-five."

"Doyle's meeting Bushy at five o'clock, and when he comes in from canoeing, he always likes to shower and change clothing. He said on his note that he'd be home at three o'clock. . . . Now I'm going to start worrying again."

"Wendy, you can't go through life worrying," he remonstrated. "We live in an age when there are sudden fatalities on the freeway and madmen with guns in the supermarket—" He winced as he heard an ominous howl from Cabin Five. It started as a growl and ended in a shriek that chilled the blood. It was Koko's death howl, and he was never wrong.

"Excuse me," he said. "Koko's letting me know something's amiss."

He ran to the cabin and phoned the inn, tracking Nick down in the basement.

"Nick, can you drop everything and come down here? Doyle Underhill hasn't returned from canoeing, and I have reason to believe he's in trouble. Could you and I take an outboard upstream? . . . Bring your cell phone."

Then he phoned Cabin One. "Hannah, are you busy? Doyle hasn't returned from canoeing, and he's late for an important appointment. It doesn't look good. Nick Bamba and I are going up the creek to investigate. Could you go over to reassure Wendy? She's getting nervous. But don't let her know that we think it's serious."

Koko was harnessed and ready to go by the time Nick came running down the back road. Qwilleran, with the cat on his shoulder met him at the boat shed. They set out in an aluminum rowboat with Nick handling the motor in the stern and the other two in the prow, peering ahead in the green tunnel of overhanging branches. Koko was quiet. Even ducks and leaping fish and squawking crows had no interest for him.

"How long has he been gone?" Nick asked.

"Left early this morning. Wendy was asleep. Left a note saying he wouldn't go ashore and would be back by three."

"How far up does he usually paddle?"

"Never mentioned it. Far enough to get good wildlife photos. Do you think there's danger in going ashore, Nick?"

"You wouldn't get me into that jungle!"

"It had a mesmerizing effect on Doyle."

"If we find the slightest clue, we call the sheriff," Nick said. "They'll need a description of the missing person. What would you say?"

"Six feet, medium build, late twenties, clean-shaven, short dark hair. For canoeing he wears blue jeans, white T-shirt, sometimes a blue denim jacket, always a bright yellow baseball cap."

"They couldn't ask better than that, Qwill. We've got a great sheriff's department—with helicopter, search-and-rescue dog, and mounted posse—all volunteers. They can put as many as twenty riders in the field, men and women."

After a while Koko began to wriggle on Qwilleran's shoulder.

"Please! No claws!" Qwilleran requested.

"Yow-w-w!"

"That means we're getting warm."

Ahead, the waterway narrowed, where uprooted trees had fallen into the stream.

Beyond was a flash of yellow, visible through the branches.

"Canoe!" yelled Qwilleran.

It had been dragged up onto the bank, which was two feet above creek level. Stashed underneath it were the paddle, a jacket and a knapsack.

"Call his name," Nick said.

Using what he called his Carnegie Hall voice, Qwilleran shouted "Doyle!"

"Yow-ow-ow!" echoed Koko.

"Shut up!" Qwilleran shouted again, while muzzling the cat with his hand.

There was no answer from the woods, only a silence that seemed twice as empty as before. . . . "Call the sheriff, Nick."

On the cell phone the innkeeper called the sheriff. One of his guests was missing. We suspect foul play. Was last seen canoeing upstream on Black Creek. The canoe (yellow) was found beached, along with paddle and knapsack, three miles south of Nutcracker Inn. Site could be identified by uprooted trees overhanging the water—also grove of black walnuts on the bank—also eagle's nest on top of highest pine tree.

Nick told them he would be back at the inn's boat shed in ten minutes with the canoeist's knapsack and jacket to provide a scent for the search dog.

The two men and the cat were quiet as their boat putt-putted back downstream. They had done all they could do.

The difference was that Nick believed there was hope; Qwilleran had heard Koko's death howl.

At the boat shed he left Nick to work with the deputies, while he hustled Koko back to the cabin.

First he phoned Cabin One; there was no answer. Hannah might still be with Wendy, but he phoned Cabin Three and drew a blank. Hannah's car was gone from the parking area, but the Underhills' SUV was in its usual slot. Could the two women be having dinner together?

It was five o'clock—when Bushy and Doyle were to meet—and he phoned the art center.

"Hey, where's our boy?" Bushy demanded. "I'm all set up here and ready to go!"

Qwilleran described the circumstances, as far as anyone knew.

"They'll find him," Bushy said with confidence. "Remember the time Junior Goodwinter was missing. They found him—broken leg—but not till the next day."

Qwilleran murmured the proper words, but he had heard Koko's howl, and there was no mistaking it.

"Excuse me, Bushy. Someone's coming." He had heard the car motor with the whirring squeal of a faulty fan belt. Hannah was driving into the parking area.

He went out to meet her. "Hannah, you should have Olsen's mechanic look at your fan belt, or you could find yourself in trouble! Where's Wendy?"

"In the hospital. I feel so sorry for that girl! Let's go in, and I'll tell you about it."

They sat on the porch, and he asked, "What happened after I asked you to go and sit with her?"

"Well, I made a pot of chamomile tea—good for calming the nerves—and took it over there. She was lying on the sofa and she said she didn't feel well. She said her arms felt numb. I phoned the office, and Lori called 911. The ambulance was there in no time! They took her to Pickax General, and I followed in my car."

Qwilleran said, "We heard the siren when we were chugging upstream. We had no idea it was headed for Cabin Three. How did she feel about going to the hospital?"

"She was composed and organized. Wanted to be sure she had her health insurance cards. Asked me to pack her robe and slippers—and leave a note for Doyle. Told me to phone her mother in Cleveland and charge the call to Cabin Three."

Qwilleran nodded. That sounded like Wendy—very thoughtful.

"What did they say at the hospital?"

"I hung around in the family waiting room until Dr. Diane came out and said everything was under control. On my way back I stopped at the office to report, and they told me that Doyle's disappearance is serious. I feel terrible about it! Will it be on the eleven o'clock newscast?"

"Only that the sheriff has authorized an

all-out search for a missing person in a wooded area. But if there's any hard news, Nick Bamba will get it first. He has connections in the sheriff's department."

When Qwilleran returned to Cabin Five, Yum Yum was asleep on the blue cushion, but Koko was keeping watch on the sofa, guarding the video of *Pirates* and the Trollope volume that Qwilleran had been reading—a Victorian novel about a scheming young woman who married for money, knowing that her bridegroom had not long to live.

By eleven o'clock it was dark, and searchlights could be seen bouncing off the clouds.

chapter fourteen

Qwilleran slept uneasily Wednesday night, burdened with knowledge he could not share. While others hoped and prayed for Doyle's rescue, he knew that the photographer was dead. And he knew—or thought he knew—that it was no accident. Many times he had heard Koko's blood curdling cry of distress, and it always meant murder. Yet how could the cat know? Qwilleran found himself stroking his moustache repeatedly and telling himself: It's only a hunch.

The Siamese had apparently slept well. They were up and about early, making subtle reminders that a new day had dawned. They pounced on his middle; Koko yelled fortissimo in his ear; Yum Yum found it amusing to bite his nose, ever so gently.

The seven o'clock newscast offered no further details about the search for a missing person. He walked up to the inn, hoping that Nick's connections at the courthouse would net some inside information. As for the day's mail, it had not yet been picked up at the post office. Qwilleran was in no hurry to see his postcard; Polly's rambles with Walter were suddenly less troubling than the fate of the photographer. He had a quick breakfast and returned to the creek without waiting for the mail. He was in time to meet a motorcycle messenger delivering a package from John Bushland. The accompanying note read:

Qwill—I stayed in the lab until I got all the rest of Doyle's stuff printed. Here's everything. Better you should have it. You'll know what to do with it. God! I hope they find that guy! I was going to take him and Wendy out on my boat this weekend. About these prints—some are very good (I like the one with the two squirrels) and some are not so good, but that's to be expected. Also some nice portraits of Wendy and some snapshots taken at a picnic, with you eating a hot dog. I called Barter. He's canceling.

Bushy

The eight-by-ten prints filled three flat yellow boxes. Qwilleran took them out to the porch. Now he would discover if it had really been a good idea to include Doyle in *The Beauty of Moose County.*

The first print in the first box was the two squirrels, photographed in profile, sitting on a tree stump face-to-face, like two elder statesmen in conference, their bushy tales arched in perfect symmetry. What were they discussing? The nut situation?

They were in the foreground, with the forest as a backdrop. Doyle had obviously used a telephoto lens.

A rumble in Koko's throat interrupted these ruminations. It was a feline alarm system that announced anyone approaching the premises, friend or foe. (Qwilleran regarded Koko as a battery-operated electronic detection device disguised as a Siamese—very few on the market—used extensively by the military—might eventually replace dogs.)

In this case, the suspected individual was Hannah Hawley, walking more briskly than usual.

Qwilleran went out to meet her, first replacing the covers on the yellow boxes; he knew Koko's fondness for glossy photoprints. "Sorry, old boy," he said. "These are for viewing, not tasting."

"Any news?" were her first words.

"Nothing."

"Wendy's mom arrives at the airport at five P.M., and I made a reservation for her at the Friendship Inn." It was a motel on the Pickax medical campus catering to the families of patients.

"Come onto the porch and have a glass of bottled water."

As soon as Hannah sat down, Yum Yum was in her lap, turning around three times before settling down. Koko jumped to the table and sat guarding the yellow boxes.

"The reason I'm here," she said as soon as the glasses of water were served, "is to tell you the latest from Cabin Two. Marge came over this morning—she never does that!—and asked if I could spare any milk for Danny. Joe was supposed to take her shopping last night, but something else came up. She seemed hungover—or doped by the medication she claims to be taking. . . . Qwill, when someone sings a flat note, it makes my flesh crawl, and Joe makes my flesh crawl." She hummed a melody from Gilbert & Sullivan that he recognized: *Things are seldom what they seem. / Skim milk masquerades as cream.*

"You think Joe's a phony?" He patted his moustache as Hannah's flat-note theory began to sound like his own hunch.

"Well, I talked to my relatives in the commercial fishing fleet, and they said the chartered trollers don't go out this time of year—except maybe weekends—"

"Food for thought," Qwilleran murmured.

"Well, you're probably busy . . . and I have a meat loaf in the oven."

"Yow!" said Koko.

"He knows the words 'meat loaf.' I'll send him a slice."

"Is there anything I can do for Wendy? Would flowers be in order?"

"Best thing you can do is hope and pray

that Doyle is safe. When her mother comes, I'll feel much relieved."

"Should I pick her up at the airport and deliver her to the Friendship Inn?"

"That would be very kind of you, Qwill."

"What's her name?"

"Wendy's maiden name was Satterlee."

Hannah went home to her meat loaf, and Qwilleran thought, If Joe didn't go fishing every day, as he claimed, what exactly was he doing? Prospecting for gold illegally? Was Hackett his partner—or competitor? Did Joe conk him on the head, throw him in the creek, and steal his car? The trunk was probably filled with gold rocks. But who drove it away? A third person must have driven it out of the state and switched the license plates.

It was time to stop inventing a scenario and dress for the MCCC luncheon. He would wear the gray polo shirt and slacks combination that accentuated his pepper-and-salt moustache—along with his summer jacket in the Mackintosh tartan. It always drew admiring glances, and although he exhibited nonchalance, he was not averse to admiring glances. Polly had said he should wear more gray, because it made his eyes look gray. . . . This bit of trivia he always remembered when dressing. (Vanity! Vanity!) Nevertheless, when he arrived at the inn, both Cathy and Lori told him he looked wonderful. The postcard he picked up was "Independence Hall" again. The message read:

Dear Qwill—All this and Greenfield Village, too! Acres and acres of history! Home soon. Wish you could meet Walter. You'd like him.

Love, Polly

Qwilleran huffed into his moustache. Walter was beginning to sound like a member of the family.

The foyer was filled with men and women heading for the private dining room—exchanging loud greetings, hearty handshakes, even hugs! It was surprising that the prospect of lunch at the Nutcracker could inspire such a festive mood. Especially since they would be getting only chicken potpie. Qwilleran waited until they were all seated around the long tables perpendicular to the speaker's table. Nell met him with effusive greetings. "You look wonderful, Qwill—but you always do!" She escorted him to the head table, where he was seated between a buxom woman with dyed red hair and an elderly man with a goatee and one gold earring. Their names were not familiar, although they knew his. As a columnist he was accustomed to this one-sided acquaintance.

Still, their friendliness, flamboyant modes of dress, and occasional shrieks of laughter seemed to him somewhat . . . unscholarly.

Then Nell tapped a water glass with a spoon and called the meeting to order. "Welcome to the annual tri-county luncheon of the Moustache Cup Collectors Club!"

Qwilleran gulped. How could he have made such a miscalculation? While keeping up a conversation with the red hair and the goatee, he tried to rework his limerick.

Nell was saying, "We are privileged to have as our speaker the leading authority on the collectibles so near and dear to our hearts." (Applause.) "And our distinguished guest-of-honor is the newspaper columnist whose wit and wisdom brighten our lives every Tuesday and Friday." (More applause—a trifle louder and more enthusiastic, Qwilleran noted with misgiving.) "How much time did he have to compose a moustache cup limerick? Moustache, dash, panache.

Nell was saying, "But first, let us relax and enjoy the delicious lunch that the chef has prepared especially for us!" (Applause again. Did they know it would be only chicken potpie?)

Hoping to pick up inspiration for his limerick, Qwilleran did what journalists do: He asked questions and listened to answers.

Moustaches, he learned, always increased in popularity following a war. The first moustache cup was introduced in England in the 1800s. Men waxed their moustaches and, when drinking hot tea, found the wax melting and running down the chin, or dripping into the beverage. The moustache cup—with a hole through which to sip—should not be confused with the shaving mug, which has three holes.

The man to Qwilleran's left claimed to have about fifty moustache cups; he had lost count. The woman to his right had just acquired a lustreware cup with hand-painted yellow roses. Nell said she specialized in cups with inscriptions, such as "Dear Papa, I love you best."

They talked about potter's marks, fakes, and such rare items as a three-legged kettle-shaped cup, and a left-handed sterling silver spoon for sipping soup.

After the chicken potpie and broccoli salad and before the dessert, the closed doors to the room opened slowly, and Nick Bamba slipped into the room. He found Qwilleran and whispered in his ear before making a quick exit.

"No!" Qwilleran responded more loudly than he intended.

He went to where Nell was sitting, whispered in her ear, then hurried from the room.

Nick was waiting in the hallway. "It was on the air: Body of missing person found in Black Forest—name withheld—cause of death not yet known—"

"That means they know but they're not telling. How did you find out he was shot?"

"Called my contact in the sheriff's office. He didn't know if wolves reached the body before the search party did."

"I don't want to know. . . . Was his camera gone?"

"That wasn't mentioned. Was it an expensive one?"

"More likely the exposed film would be more important to the shooter. Sounds to me like another gold prospector, afraid of having his illegal operation photographed. This is a tragic situation for Wendy. What can be done?"

"We thought her doctor should be given the facts, so she can act in the best interests of her patient. Lori called Dr. Diane."

"You did right, Nick. I'm picking up Wendy's mother at the airport, and I'll tell her only what the police have released to the media."

"Sorry I interrupted your party, Qwill."

"Don't be sorry. I'm glad you did."

Qwilleran took the short cut to Cabin Five, via the back road, and made a strong cup of coffee. The cats sensed his preoccupation and were quiet—but not for long. Koko started jumping on and off the furniture, all the while talking to himself. Someone was coming!

It was Trent, the porter from the inn, delivering a large silver-wrapped cube topped with a huge silver bow. He said, "They were going to give you this at the luncheon, but you left early."

"Is someone giving me a bowling ball?"

"Or a mummified head," said Trent with a grin.

It was, as he had feared, a moustache cup and saucer—but not the lustreware with hand-painted yellow roses. The set was earthenware, with a decent-sized mug and a good handle for gripping. What made it rare, he later learned, was the advertising on both mug and saucer, promoting men's coats, trousers and vests made to order with perfect fit guaranteed. A sketch showing a frock-coated tailor and a top-hatted customer suggested that the set was early twentieth century.

A note from Nell said, "We were horrified to hear about your friend. We can understand your sudden departure. But I said some nice things about you, and all the members send their condolences. Here is a token of our esteem."

He was scribbling a thank-you note when he was distracted by the sound of a car with a faulty fan belt. He recognized it as Hannah's vehicle, and he was not surprised when she phoned him, saying breathlessly, "Have you heard the news, Qwill?"

"What news?" he asked.

She repeated the WPKX bulletin, adding, "It pains me to think how Wendy will react. Thank God her mom is on the way here." Then, in a confidential tone, she said, "You know, Wendy's parents didn't want her to marry Doyle. They thought he was too self-centered."

"What can one say? It happens in the best of families."

"I called the hospital, and the nurse said

Wendy is in stable condition. . . . Well, I guess that's all I have to say."

"That's not all I have to say, Hannah. You'd better have your fan belt checked. Your motor doesn't sound good."

Koko was jumping on and off the table where the yellow boxes were stacked. He knew what they contained, and he liked nothing better than to lick the emulsion on the surface of a glossy photograph.

Qwilleran himself had no heart for looking at Doyle's prints. Eventually he and Bushy would choose the best and proceed with the art book. Koko was sniffing the yellow boxes; he could detect a photograph the way a squirrel could detect a nut buried six inches underground. Qwilleran spent a restless hour or two until it was time to leave for the airport.

The shuttle flight that brought passengers from the large airports to Moose County was called "The Wright

Brothers Special" by local wags. Its unofficial slogan was *Better Than Nothing.*

Qwilleran was there when the plane fell out of the sky and bounced up to the terminal. Men and women carrying briefcases or shopping bags virtually tumbled down the gangway in their eagerness to be on the ground again. Last to appear was a woman wearing a business suit and a tailored hat and carrying a small piece of smart luggage. She looked more like the chairman of the board, composed and very much in charge and not at all like someone's mom.

"Mrs. Satterlee? I'm Jim Qwilleran," he said. "I'm to drive you to the hospital."

"How is Wendy?" she asked quickly.

"In stable condition and having very good care. May I take your luggage? My car is over there."

There was no small talk about the weather or the eccentricities of the shuttle service, but when he turned the key in the ignition of the van, she said, "Now! What do you know about the circumstances preceding Wendy's attack? She had been phoning me twice a week but may not have been telling me everything. She said they were having a wonderful time."

"So it appeared, but at a dinner party one night—after too much wine, perhaps—she and Doyle had a family spat. She didn't want him to go into the woods to photograph wildlife, saying there were bears, poisonous snakes and rabid foxes. The next day, after he had gone upstream in his canoe, Wendy came to my cabin and apologized for the outburst; she said she was worried sick."

"She's a worrier, no doubt about it," said her mother, "but she's supposed to avoid stress because of a congenital heart condition. Doyle is aware of the situation and should not upset her unnecessarily. I gathered, however, that they were leaving Black Creek early and going to another resort for a few days."

"That was the plan," Qwilleran said, "but yesterday he went canoeing for one last time and didn't return. We filed a Missing Persons report, and the sheriff launched an all-out search. Wendy was rushed to the hospital."

"Our cardiologist wants her brought

home to Cleveland as soon as she can travel, even if it means chartering a plane."

"That's something for you to discuss with her doctor, Diane Lanspeak. You'll be staying at an inn on the grounds of the hospital."

Then Mrs. Satterlee asked the question that was painful to answer. "Have they found Doyle?"

He hesitated before saying, "They've found the body."

"How terrible—for Wendy! And in her condition!" There was a long pause. "What happened to him?"

Qwilleran hesitated again. "No further details have been released by the sheriff's department."

After that there was not much conversation. He pointed out the hospital—an impressive facility for a small community—and delivered his passenger to the Friendship Inn with its flower garden and benches for meditation. "Here's my phone number," he said. "Don't hesitate to call if there's anything I can do."

Later that evening—when he sat on the

porch contemplating the peaceful scene—
he asked himself questions.

At what time did Wendy express alarm
about the gunfire? (He had attributed it to
the ever-present rabbit hunters.)

At what time did Koko chill the scene
with his death-howl? (Shortly before they
all went up the creek in search of Doyle's
canoe.)

There had been another minor incident:
Koko looking out the south window of the
bunk room—and growling at a noisy vehicle. In an effort at humor, that was lost on
the growler, Qwilleran had said to him,
"That's only a bad muffler. You should
check your own muffler."

At what time did that incident occur?
That was Joe's truck—coming home early
and then going out again.

chapter fifteen

G. Allen Barter phoned Cabin Five
early Friday morning—too early.

"Yes?" Qwilleran replied sleepily.

"Qwill! The WPKX newscast says the
body of the missing person has been
found in the Black Forest."

"Right."

"But according to the grapevine, it's a
homicide case."

"Right. But don't spread it around. The
police have their reasons for doing what
they do."

"Do you realize," said the attorney, "that
two guests of an inn owned by the K Fund
have been murdered in a conservancy
owned by the K Fund? And in less than
two weeks! What's going on?"

"I have a fairly good idea: Same
'perp' . . . two different motives."

"Any idea who the perpetrator is?"

Qwilleran patted his moustache smugly. "I have a hunch, but right now I'm concerned about the survivors. Wendy Underhill is hospitalized with a heart condition and can't be told about her husband's fate. Her mother, who flew up here from Cleveland yesterday, knows that his body was found but not that he was murdered. Doyle's father is on his way here. They face problems and difficult decisions—in a strange environment. Let's help these people. Put your good Samaritans on the case!" That was Qwilleran's flip cognomen for Barter's assistants who specialized in social services and investigation.

"I agree," said Barter. "Who are the principals and where can they be found?"

"Wendy is in Pickax General, and her doctor is Diane Lanspeak. Her mother is Mrs. Satterlee, staying at the Friendship Inn—a strong, sensible businesswoman. Doyle's father should be met at the airport at five o'clock and taken to the Friendship Inn; I don't know anything about him, but Mrs. Satterlee could fill you in."

Barter asked, "What's your feeling about the art book?"

"I think we should go ahead with it as a kind of memorial to a dedicated photographer." If he had been less dedicated, Qwilleran thought, he'd be alive today!

Pickax was only a twenty-minute drive from Black Creek, but psychologically it was a day's journey. Instead of faxing his Friday column, he took his copy to the office of the *Moose County Something* and threw it on Junior Goodwinter's desk.

"Back from vacation, Qwill?" asked the managing editor.

"What vacation? I haven't had a relaxing moment in the last two weeks."

"How would you like to cover the reenactment tomorrow night?"

"Assign Roger," Qwilleran said. "He lives on the shore and could use the overtime. And he knows the lumberjack lingo. You should go yourself; it would be educational. Do you know what it means to get your teeth fixed?"

"No. What?"
"Go and see!"

From there he went to Lois's Luncheonette to treat himself to breakfast. She served superlative eggs-over-lightly with American fries! Lois Inchpot was a buxom, bossy, hard-working woman, whose lunchroom had been a shabby downtown landmark for years and years. Her customers regularly took up a collection when new equipment was needed for the kitchen. And when the dingy walls needed repainting, they volunteered their time and came in on the weekend. To be one of Lois's "family" was a mark of distinction, and although Qwilleran never soiled his hands, he bought the paint.

When Lois saw him through the kitchen pass-through she yelled, "Where've you been? Lost your taste for apple pie?"

"I've been out of town, but I thought about your apple pie constantly!"

"For that you get a free cup of coffee. Help yourself."

It was a sociable place. There was loud conversation between tables and—in lowered voices—the best gossip in town. When the other customers saw their favorite newsman, they shouted:

"How does it feel to be back in civilization after livin' with all them squirrels?"

"Do any fishin' in the creek, Mr. Q?"

"Did they find the guy that got lost in the woods?"

Qwilleran looked at his watch. "Let's tune in the news and find out."

The WPKX announcer said:

"The motorist arrested by Pickax police officers yesterday afternoon will be arraigned today on charges of driving while impaired, failing to stop for a school bus, and causing damage to city property. The students, being bussed home from Pickax middle school, were wearing seat belts, and there were no personal injuries. Both vehicles sustained damage when the white station wagon sideswiped the bus."

At a table near Qwilleran a man wearing mechanic's coveralls said, "That was my next-door neighbor. His wife's fit to be tied! It was a brand new station wagon—not a week old yet."

"Shut up! We wanna hear the news!" someone yelled.

The announcer was saying, ". . . who jumped or fell from the Old Stone Bridge was pulled from the Black Creek early this morning by the sheriff's rescue squad. They responded to a 911 call by a fisherman on the bridge who heard the splash and reported it on his cell phone. The unidentified body was that of a young woman—"

"Heard the splash!" yelled the mechanic. "Why didn't he jump in and save her?"

"Shut up!"

From the loud speaker came the evasive newsbite: ". . . whose body was found yesterday in the Black Forest. No further information has been released by the sheriff's department."

"Somethin' fishy about that," the mechanic said. "Somethin' they're not tellin'!"

 At the florist shop he asked a question of the friendly assistant whose name he could never remember; she had long blond hair—and blue eyes filled with perpetual wonder. Cindy? Mindy? Candy? "Are you going to be able to fill my order?"

"They went out on the truck first thing, Mr. Q. We had them shipped from Chicago. They're beautiful!"

At the converted apple barn that was the official dwelling of the Siamese and himself, he packed his kilt, shoulder plaid, brogues and all the other paraphernalia for Scottish Night. It occurred to him that the vast building had a peculiar hush when there was no cat flesh in residence.

Then it was back to the Nutcracker Inn to pick up Polly's postcard. On a sideboard in the foyer stood a large silver ice bucket filled with daffodils—a half-bushel of them, he estimated. Guests were viewing them with awe.

"Magnificent massing! . . . Thrilling yellows! . . . Such happy flower faces!" they gushed. "Who is Anne Mackintosh Qwilleran?"

A small tasteful card dedicated the floral display to her memory. Qwilleran scuttled into the office, hoping not to be recognized.

Both Bambas were in the office—one at the computer and one at the coffee urn.

Lori said, "They're gorgeous, Qwill! Do you approve of the silver ice bucket?"

Nick said, "You went all-out, brother! What's the occasion? Have a cuppa?"

Qwilleran accepted a mug of coffee—and a chair—and explained, "This is my mother's birthday. She's been gone more than thirty years, but I still remember how she recited her birthday poem every year: 'I wandered lonely as a cloud / That floats on high o'er vales and hills, / When all at once I saw a crowd, / A host, of golden daffodils'!"

"What a lovely idea!" Lori exclaimed. "I'm going to find a birthday poem! Maybe by Emily Dickinson. Do you have one, Qwill?"

"No, but if I did, it would be Kipling: *If I can keep my head while all about me are losing theirs.*"

Nick said, "Mine would be: *Over the hill to the poorhouse.*"

"Isn't he terrible!" Lori said, gazing fondly at her husband.

Qwilleran took his postcard and left, sneaking a look at the picture. They were still at the Henry Ford Museum & Greenfield Village. "They" instead of "she."

The message read:

Dear Qwill—Walter and I are having our farewell dinner Friday night. I'll arrive Saturday on the 5 P.M. shuttle if the repair crew doesn't run out of scotch tape.

Love, Polly

The humor was somewhat giddy—for the Polly he knew. Had Walter introduced her to Fish House punch? It was an early American favorite. George Washington drank it. He huffed into his moustache.

The Siamese were glad to see him— and why not? They had not been served their noon repast of crunchies.

"We're checking out tomorrow," he told them as they crunched.

Within minutes Hannah Hawley phoned,

as if she had been watching for his van to pull into the lot. She spoke in a hushed and hurried voice. "Qwill! Strange development! Could I come over for a minute?"

"Of course! Take two!"

She had hung up before his quip reached her, and she came along the footpath at a trot. "I left Danny sleeping, and I don't want him to wake up and find himself alone." She declined a glass of fruit juice.

Into Qwilleran's mind flashed the newscast . . . a splash in the creek . . . the unidentified body . . . a young woman. He said, "Calm down, Hannah. Take a deep breath. Start from the beginning."

"Well . . . about eight o'clock this morning I was just waking up, and did the first thing I always do—I unlock the front door and step out on the screened porch for a few deep breaths. Imagine my surprise when I saw Danny sitting out there, looking at a picture book! I remarked that he was up bright and early, and asked if his mom knew he was here. He said, 'She's gone away. She told me to go and see Auntie Hannah if she ever went away. I haven't had any breakfast.' He was wearing the blue T-shirt I'd given him, and he showed me something in the pocket."

She seemed unable to go on, and Qwilleran said, "You'd better have a glass of fruit juice." He waited until she had taken a few sips before asking her, "What was in the pocket?"

"Some money—and a note. I brought it to show you."

She handed over a scribbled message on a square of greasy paper that might have come from a box of cookies.

> Take care of Danny.
> Tell him his mom is sick—
> We have no place to go—
> I hate my life—
> Joe is a bad bad man—
> Danny will be better off without me—
>
> Marge

"That poor woman!" Hannah said, clutching her throat to control her emotions. "Homeless! Addicted to alcohol— maybe drugs. Then I heard the newscast, and I knew it was Marge. 'There but for the grace of God go I.' . . . Do you know who said that?"

"I'm afraid not." With a shudder he recalled how close he had come to the same condition . . . once upon a time, eons ago.

Now Hannah had given way to sobs, and he brought her a box of tissues.

"I wanted to help her," Hannah said, "but she kept to herself always. I think she was afraid of Joe."

Qwilleran wondered, did Marge know he was a gold-digger and not a deep-sea fisherman? Did she know he'd murdered twice to protect his turf?

Sniffing and dabbing her eyes, she said, "I'd love to adopt Danny! My grandson in Florida is his age. The Scottens and Hawleys have a good family life. I was trained as a teacher. But . . . he's a 'John Doe.' We don't know his name, or where he's from. If the county gets hold of him, he'll spend his life with different foster families. I don't know anything about the law, but I've seen it happen to other orphans—"

Qwilleran interrupted her torrent of thoughts. "Hannah, the K Fund can handle this. They have a battery of investigators and advisers who'll work this out in Danny's best interests."

"Is that a fact?" she asked. "The county—"

"Forget the county. They're always glad to work with the K Fund. Put on a cheerful face and go home to Danny, and I'll make a phone call and start the wheels turning."

She hesitated. "Maybe I should tell you what I did. As soon as Danny fell asleep, I went next door to collect his clothes and things. There was hardly anything to collect. He doesn't even have a toothbrush or sleeping pajamas! . . . And listen to this, Qwill! There wasn't a single sign that Joe had ever been there!"

Except fingerprints, Qwilleran thought.

After Hannah had gone back to Cabin One, and after the Good Samaritans had been alerted, Qwilleran phoned Nick. He said, "Tell your friends at the sheriff's office to get out the yellow tape. One of your cabins down here at the creek should be searched. I suggest you come down here for a conference."

While waiting for the manager, he made
a quick scan of Doyle's photos—the ones
in the box that Bushy had marked "mis-
cellaneous." They were typical vacation
mementos. The Shipwreck Tavern in
Mooseville, commercial fishing wharves,
the Hotel Booze in Brrr, flower gardens at
the state prison, the historic Nutcracker
Inn, Wendy feeding squirrels, the picturesque Old Stone Bridge, and picnickers eating hot dogs. That was the one he
had been looking for.

"It's always at the bottom of the pile," he
told Koko, who was watching the process
with a superior air. "So why didn't you tell
me to start at the bottom?"

When Nick arrived, Qwilleran offered him
a beer, told him to sit on the porch, and
gave him an eight-by-ten photo of a picnic group. "Recognize any of these,
Nick?"

"Well, the one with a moustache works
for the newspaper . . . and I know Mrs.
Hawley . . . and I think the one in a baseball cap is Joe Thompson."

Qwilleran said, "He may have registered
under that name, but I suspect it's an

alias . . . and I suspect he's gone fugitive after killing Doyle Underhill. The police said that Doyle was shot about four o'clock on Wednesday. Shortly after that Joe's truck drove in, stayed a short time, and drove off—abandoning the woman and child who shared the cabin. . . . Incidentally, did you hear the newscast about a suicide in Black Creek?"

"I heard something—"

"I think the unidentified body will match the scrawny woman in the picnic photo. She left a suicide note in the pocket of her son's T-shirt, calling Joe a bad bad man."

Nick, father of three, said, "Where's the kid?"

"Mrs. Hawley is looking after him and would like to adopt him."

Nick stood up to leave. "I think Lori was right, Qwill. The Nutcracker is jinxed!"

Now Qwilleran had to shift gears—from the somber reality of the creekside situation to the festive celebration of Scottish Night. His training in theater had taught him how to "make an adjustment," and a long ride on his Silverlight helped. The steady rhythm of pedaling, the therapy of deep breathing, and the serenity of secondary roads—all combined to put him in a propitious mood.

The Siamese—who had panicked the first time they saw him in kilt and knee socks—were two cool cats when he confronted them in full regalia. He promised to bring them a taste of haggis.

Traffic was heavy in downtown Black Creek, and MCCC students provided valet parking so that guests in Highland dress could enter the building in style.

They were greeted at the door by Ernie Kemple and his partner, Anne Munroe. The red, blue, gold and green of clan tartans moved among the twenty booths of antiques and collectibles. A bagpiper was piping, and a young woman danced the Highland fling with seeming weightlessness. Guests drank punch and Scotch and nibbled bridies and haggis.

Janelle Van Roop presided over the museum exhibit of Elsa's black walnut furniture and handed out copies of Qwilleran's tale of the three cracked mirrors. The

painting of her great-grandmother, described in the "Qwill Pen," could be seen
in the locked case.

All the prominent Scots were there:
MacWhannell, Abernethy, Ogilvie, Camp-
bell, MacMurchie and more. "Where's
Polly Duncan?" was the question that
Qwilleran heard on every side.

He was talking with Ernie Kemple when
a clock in one of the booths announced
the hour.

"Cuckoo! Cuckoo!"

"Excuse me," Qwilleran said, "I'm being
paged."

He tracked it down to a booth specializing in clocks. It was exactly like the one
stolen from the Limburger mansion—or so
he thought. It was a masterpiece of carving: a rustic hut nestled in a bower of
leaves, with a swinging pendulum and
three long weights ending in pinecones.
He wanted to demand, "Where did you get
it?" Instead, he asked, "Do you know its
provenance?"

The dealer said:

"Hand-carved in Germany's Black Forest probably early twentieth century—

linden wood—mechanically operated by weights in the old style—eight-day movement. Cuckoo pops out on the hour, but there's a way to shut him off at night. Some people like to hear it at night; they say it doesn't disturb—only reassures."

Qwilleran thought, It would drive me crazy, and the cats would climb up the wall and kill it. It was not for himself, however. He inquired casually, "What are you asking for it?"

"Three hundred, but if I thought it would have a good home, I'd let it go for two-seventy-five."

"Oh," Qwilleran said and started to walk away.

"Two-fifty, sir!"

"Hmmm . . . It's for a gift. Do you have a box? Nothing fancy."

"I can find one out back; just give me ten minutes. . . . Will it be check or credit card, sir?"

Qwilleran walked among the crowd, chatting with friends.

Nell Abernethy said, "Don't tell anyone, but the secret of my black walnut pie is maple syrup and a dash of vinegar to cut the sweetness."

Ernie Kemple lowered his booming voice and confided, "My ex-wife is asking for a reconciliation. . . . No way!"

Burgess Campbell, blind from birth, was there with Alexander, his guide dog. "I come for the fellowship and because Alexander is hooked on haggis. Have you bought anything Qwill?"

"Yes, I picked up a couple of scamadiddles at a reasonable price." It was a private joke between the two men, and Burgess roared with laughter, causing the dog to nudge him. "Trouble with Alex—he has no sense of humor."

Qwilleran picked up his clock and drove back to the creek, where he knocked on the back door of Cabin One.

"Qwill, you look wonderful!" Hannah cried when she saw his Highland attire. "Come in! What are you carrying?"

He said, "I've found the cuckoo clock that Gus Limburger promised to your nephew. It was stolen from the mansion, you remember."

"Aubrey will be so happy! Where did you find it?"

"That's classified information. . . . How's Danny?"

"He's asleep. I bought him a toothbrush and showed him how to brush his teeth and say his prayers. Then I sang 'Danny Boy,' changing the words a bit. He's a good boy. He ate his carrots when I told him to. . . . Won't you come in, Qwill?"

"Thanks, but I have to go home and feed the cats."

He could hear Koko's yowling coming from Cabin Five. That cat recognized the sound of Qwilleran's motor a block away! The yowling stopped when the brown van stopped at the back door. It had been daylight when Qwilleran left; now the interior was dark. He flicked the wall switch. There—scattered all over the floor—were Doyle's photos!

"Bad cat!" he shouted, clapping his palms together in a loud reprimand. It sent the guilty Koko flying about the room. Yum

Yum, perched on the TV, watched the performance in dismay.

"Out! Out!" Qwilleran opened the door to the screened porch, and the two of them rushed out, willingly, to enjoy the mysteries of the night.

He changed into a jumpsuit and crawled about the floor, collecting prints and loading them into the yellow boxes without bothering to sort the categories. That could be done later. Only one photo did he reserve—another shot of the picnickers eating hot dogs.

He hoped the cat had not drooled on any of them. His saliva and raspy tongue had damaged glossy photos in the past.

In daylight it would be easier to look for rough spots.

chapter sixteen

Moving day! Qwilleran surprised the cats by rising early and feeding them a smorgasbord of leftovers from the refrigerator. He, himself, drove to the inn for one more memorable breakfast and then to Olsen's to buy gas and check the oil and tires. He also showed Jake Olsen an eight-by-ten photo, asking, "Do you recognize the fellow in a baseball cap?"

"Sure! He comes around to gas up his truck and order take-outs from the lunch counter. Haven't seen him for a couple of days, though. . . . And hey! He's the guy who was trying to hire extras for a logging movie. It fell through, but he decided to stay and do some deep-sea fishing."

"Hope you have a good summer, Jake. I'm moving back to Pickax, but I'll drop in once in a while to have my air pressure checked—for old times' sake. And good luck with the reenactment!"

Olsen's was around the corner from the Antique Village, and Qwilleran stopped there to ask questions: Did they consider Scottish Night a success? Did the dealers sell much? Which was more popular—the fruit punch or the Scotch? How did people react to the exhibit of Elsa's black walnut furniture? (The answers to the first three were: yes . . . no . . . fifty-fifty.)

"But they flipped over Elsa's furniture," Janelle said, "and some of the women want to start an Elsa club—not just another gossip circle, but a discussion group about women's problems, the decisions they have to make, today's attitudes and so forth."

Qwilleran said it might make copy for the "Qwill Pen" after it got started.

When he returned to Cabin Five, he found that the Siamese had devised their own farewell: All the built-in drawers on nylon rollers were open—all twenty-three of them! Who could say that animals have no sense of humor?

All three residents of the converted apple barn were glad to be home. The Siamese raced up and down the ramp that connected the three balconies.

Qwilleran, after unpacking, went to Toodle's Market to buy frozen macaroni and cheese for himself and boned turkey for the cats.

After that he moved them to the screened gazebo while he sorted Doyle's photos into the original categories. There were only two prints damaged by Koko's saliva and raspy tongue, but they were important shots. How did the cat know? What was he trying to say? Or was it coincidental?

Qwilleran kept an eye on his watch; he was scheduled to meet Polly at five o'clock. The shuttle was never on time, but waiting for it was half the fun; groundlings bantered in Moose County style:

"I hear the skeeter-meter is up ten points."

"The stores have run out of insect repellent."

"The tourists are getting it on the black market."

"Here she comes!" A small speck had appeared in the sky to the south.

"Can you see if she's still got both wings?"

A shout went up when the wheels touched down, and the meeters-and-greeters walked out on the tarmac. Polly was the last to come down the gangway, using a cane and descending carefully, her bad ankle hidden by a trouser-leg.

While other travelers were embraced as fortunate survivors, Qwilleran and Polly reserved fond greetings until later; the busybodies were always watching.

"Need a wheelchair?" he asked.

"No thanks, dear. The cane is just to command special attention."

"You're a sly one! Did you have your ankle X-rayed?"

"Yes. It's not serious."

"Where's my friend Walter?"

"I sent him back to Ohio," she said in a matter-of-fact way, leading Qwilleran to

wonder, Could she have invented him? . . .
No, she's not devious enough or creative
enough to play such a trick. . . . but it
would have been a clever one!

When her luggage was stowed in the van
and they were on the road to her Indian
Village condo, she said, "I've missed Brutus and Catta so much! I wonder if they've
missed me?"

"I know they have," Qwilleran said. "I
could tell by their look of disappointment
when I unlocked your door and went in to
cheer them up."

"I can hardly wait to see them! . . . How
was your stay at the Nutcracker?"

"Interesting. There were two murders, a
suicide and a heart attack—all guests
from Down Below, staying in the rustic
cabins along the creek."

Warily, as if suspecting a hoax, she said,
"Tell me about it."

"Well, first there was a male guest pur-
porting to be a sales representative who
was actually a gold prospector operating
illegally in the Black Forest Conservancy.
He was murdered presumably for his
forty-thousand-dollar car and a trunkful of

gold nuggets. . . . Next, there was an accomplished photographer shooting pictures of wildlife in the creek and in the woods. He was murdered presumably because another gold prospector thought his illegal activity was being photographed. . . . The photographer's young wife had a heart attack and is hospitalized. . . . Do you follow me?"

"I follow you," Polly said, "but I can't believe it!"

"Now, another guest, posing as a sport fisherman but thought to be another gold prospector, is suspected of both murders and has taken off with his truck and all personal belongings, abandoning the woman and child who have been traveling with him for reasons open to speculation. She was a sad case, apparently homeless and addicted, and she jumped off the Old Stone Bridge this morning, leaving a suicide note in the pocket of her son's T-shirt."

"Oh, Qwill!" she protested, "this sounds more like fiction than real life!"

"The next chapter is in the typewriter," he replied.

He avoided mentioning Koko's uncanny role in the drama. Polly had a practical turn of mind that squelched the idea of a cat with supranormal gifts. The fact that Koko had sixty whiskers and her beloved Brutus had only the usual forty-eight must have rankled in her maternal subconscious. Qwilleran had learned not to brag about his pets.

On arrival at her home Polly rushed indoors, and when Qwilleran carried in her luggage, he found her kneeling on the hearth rug and slavering over her two excited pets.

"I'll phone you after you've settled in," he said, "and we'll make plans for tomorrow."

Qwilleran's Siamese were not excited to see him, having seen him every day for several years. He fed them, thawed macaroni and cheese for himself, and then finished unpacking. When he carried a carton of writing materials to the studio on the first balcony, Koko followed, purring throatily as if he knew it contained those flat yellow boxes. There were also file folders, books, copy paper and soft lead pencils, but as soon as the yellow boxes were stacked on the desk, Koko moved in to huddle on them cozily—keeping them warm, so to speak.

"Don't get any ideas!" Qwilleran warned, and the cat squeezed his eyes as he did when planning a nefarious misdemeanor. "How about going out to talk to the crows?" Without waiting for an answer, he transported them to the screened gazebo.

Then he sorted the photos, looking for shots worthy of the art book: the great owl in flight, the two squirrels in conference, busy beavers, smart raccoons, a doe and her fawn drinking from the creek, and more. Only two had been damaged by Koko's slobbering, and Bushy could make new prints.

One was the skunk shot that Doyle had found comic. Here was a creature of the wild having an afternoon nap on a piece of mechanical equipment. It looked like the seat of a tractor. Perhaps the sun had warmed the metal. Perhaps the elevation gave the animal a feeling of security.

Qwilleran amused himself by composing a cutline for the photo: "If you're a skunk, you'll never be satisfied with anything else after you've had a nap in the seat of a fork-lift."

"Forklift!" he said aloud. "What's a fork-lift doing in the Black Forest?" He looked at the squirrel photo, and then he knew. He grabbed the phone and called the Brodie residence; they would be watching their regular Saturday-night movie on the VCR.

"Andy! When the flick's finished, drive over to the barn for a nightcap and a new slant on the Nutcracker case." No more needed to be said. The Brodies lived only five minutes away.

Quickly Qwilleran brought the cats in from the gazebo . . . set out Scotch and chicken liver paté on the snack bar . . . put the moustache cup on the work bar for Brodie's amusement.

 "What's that ugly thing?" were the chief's first words.

"A moustache cup. A hundred years old and very valuable. It was a gift."

Brodie grunted and sat down, pouring himself a Scotch without delay.

The Siamese immediately came forward to sniff his shoes and rub against his legs.

"They're giving me the business again," he said. "What are they up to?"

"It's your animal magnetism, Andy. . . . What film did you watch tonight?"

"Something called *Driving Miss Daisy*. It was her choice. Last Saturday night we saw a good one about a submarine. What's this in the bowl? Peanut butter?"

"It's chicken liver spread from Toodle's deli counter. You'll like it. Spread some on a cracker."

At that moment there was a shattering crash. The moustache cup had disappeared from the end of the work bar, and the culprits were peering over the edge of the bar and pondering the disaster on the quarry tile floor.

Brodie laughed until he choked. "That cat's smarter than I thought he was!"

Qwilleran said, "Wait till you see Koko's

choice of the two most interesting photos in Underhill's collection."

Brodie looked at the squirrels. "Those are tree stumps in the background! Looks as if a whole grove has been cut down! Where was this taken?"

"In the Black Forest Conservancy, where timbering is illegal. Those stumps represent a million dollars' worth of black walnut."

"How do you know?"

"I borrowed a book from Doc Abernethy. . . . Andy, we have tree pirates in the Conservancy!"

"I've heard of tree rustlers—"

"Same thing." Qwilleran looked at Koko and remembered the cat's fascination with Hannah's video. *A rollicking band of pirates we!*

Qwilleran went on. "The suspect, I believe, is an experienced woodsman. He was up here a few weeks ago and talked to Jake Olsen about hiring young huskies for a logging movie. Actually, he was probably mapping the territory and locating the best black walnuts. He would bring his own crew. A furniture-moving van was seen in the vicinity. We can guess that it brought up the chain saws and forklift . . . and the lumberjacks . . . and maybe camouflage tents. Then it hauled ten-foot logs Down Below. To expedite the robbery, they might dump them in a holding warehouse in a nearby county and return for another load. For what it's worth, the van had a Wisconsin tag and DIAMOND COMPANY logo."

Qwilleran glanced at Koko and thought about the Trollope novel they had been reading. He said, "Shortly after Underhill was shot, the suspect drove his truck up to Cabin Two and cleared out his gear, and Koko looked out the window and growled. That cat knows when people are up to no good."

Brodie grunted, then stared at the cat, who responded amiably. In the beginning the chief had scoffed at Koko's intuitive reactions and discoveries—until a detective Down Below assured him the cat was "psychic."

Now he poured another Scotch and listened to the rest of the story: how Koko had identified the first victim as a gold prospector . . . how he had known it was the man's body coming downstream and not just a six-foot log . . . how his howls had succeeded in getting them evicted from 3FF. As if he sensed that all the action was going to be down by the creek.

"Why not?" Brodie asked. "They say cats can predict earthquakes. . . . Is it okay if I give these two photos to the SBI? Off the record, they know who the suspect is. Now it's a manhunt. I'll pass along your information—but leave you out of it."

"Leave both of us out of it."

Qwilleran walked with his guest to his car.

"Nice night," Brodie said.

"Yes, I'll walk around the barn before I go indoors. Three times around is a quarter of a mile, according to the pedometer."

"Almost forgot, Qwill. My wife wanted to tell you about a thought she had. Everybody knows that Fanny Klingenschoen never gave anything away. Do you think the K Fund's generosity has Fanny turning over in her grave?"

Qwilleran chuckled. "I only know that a wise man once said three hundred years ago that money is like muck; it doesn't do any good unless you spread it around."

Before going inside to give the Siamese their bedtime snack, Qwilleran walked around the barn two times. He wondered, How much of Koko's involvement in the case has been the extrasensory perception of a cat with sixty whiskers, and how much has been coincidence? As for the cat's oblique way of communicating (operatic "pirates" suggesting tree pirates) . . . that had to be a mix of happenstance and a vivid imagination.

When he went indoors, he first had to sweep up the shards of the moustache cup. Hunting for dustpan and brush in the broom closet, he called out, "Which one of you rascals pleads guilty to the destruction of a valuable artifact?"

"Yargle!" came the reply—from a cat

yowling and swallowing at the same time. Both cats were on the snack bar. Koko was swallowing his last tongueful of chicken liver paté and Yum Yum was looking ruefully at the empty bowl.